Peter C enthusi
the loca
originally a historian, but would now classify himself as a journalist and thriller writer.

BY THE SAME AUTHOR

The Dying Trade
White Meat
The Marvellous Boy
The Empty Beach
Heroin Annie
Make Me Rich
The Winning Side

Peter Corris
THE BIG DROP
and other Cliff Hardy stories

UNWIN PAPERBACKS
Sydney London Boston

First published in Australia
by Unwin Paperbacks 1985

This book is copyright under the Berne Convention.
No reproduction without permission. All rights
reserved.

UNWIN® PAPERBACKS
Allen & Unwin Australia Pty Ltd
8 Napier St, North Sydney, NSW 2060, Australia

UNWIN PAPERBACKS
18 Park Lane, Hemel Hempstead,
Herts HP2 4TE, England

© Peter Corris 1985

National Library of Australia
Cataloguing-in-Publication entry:

Corris, Peter, 1942-.
  The big drop, and other Cliff Hardy stories.
  ISBN 0 86861 767 9.
  1. Detective and mystery stories, Australian. I.
  Title.
A823'.3

Typeset by Graphicraft Typesetters Ltd., Hong Kong
Printed by The Dominion Press-Hedges & Bell, Victoria

Contents

The Big Drop   *1*
P.I. Blues   *22*
The Arms of the Law   *40*
Tearaway   *63*
What Would You Do?   *83*
The Mongol Scroll   *104*
The Mae West Scam   *129*
Rhythm Track   *148*
The Big Pinch   *166*
Maltese Falcon   *190*

For
Matthew Kelly

The Big Drop

They found my late client, Norman Scholfield, at the bottom of a half-built office block in the city. That is, they found part of him there; the office block is destined to rise twenty-five storeys above our fair city and Norman came off the twentieth which is just a concrete shell. He'd bounced on the scaffolding a few times on the way down and this smeared and scattered him around a little. Still, my card was in pristine condition in his pants pocket, which was why Detective Sergeant Frank Parker was sitting in the client's chair in my office. The last bum on that chair was the now fairly widely distributed Norman's, but I didn't tell Frank that.

'What did you make of him?' Parker said.

I shrugged. 'Man in trouble, real or imagined. He had a delivery to make to an address and he needed protection.'

'What was he delivering?'

'Money, what else? Said he was paying off a bet.'

'You believed that?'

I shrugged again. 'People pay on bets, happens every day. Times are tough, Frank. He was a nice guy; I liked him. In this business liking the people who hire you is a bonus. He paid up like a gentleman.'

'I bet he did. Where was the delivery to?'

'Well, that's another thing—wasn't as if it was a meeting in a sewer. How about you answer a question or two before I have to give my grandmother's maiden name?'

Frank looked interested; that was what made him more agreeable than the average cop—he had more on his mind than charge sheets and beer. 'D'you know your grandmother's maiden name?'

'One of 'em, yeah. Come on, Frank. Give a bit.'

'Norman had a few convictions and a few near misses. Nothing big, nothing very bad—fraud mostly.' He grinned at me. 'People found him a nice guy.'

I let that pass. 'I didn't think he was Fred Nile. So the money was hot?'

'We don't know, we didn't find any money; but the thing is, the forensic boys noticed some dye on his hands. You know, the kind that gets on money that men with stockings over their heads take out of banks.'

I was reaching back for my wallet before he finished talking. 'He gave me a couple of hundreds; I broke one of them.' The other hundred dollar note was nestling in cosily with a couple of twenties and some others hardly worth talking about. I pulled it out and handed it to Frank. He looked at it.

'Looks clean to me. Got an envelope?'

I passed one across and he put the note in it. 'Want a receipt?'

'Bet your arse.'

'You'll have to come down to the station to get one.'

I spread my hands. 'I'll trust you. Well, let me know how it checks out.'

'Don't be funny, Cliff. Norman wasn't up there for the view, and there's too much of that tie-dyed money floating around for comfort. This is a serious matter, and I want the address you went to.'

I looked out the window while I considered it. Scholfield had commented on the view when he was in the office: 'Water view', he'd said, meaning the road repair trench that had filled up from the burst main. We'd had a few laughs and he'd paid me two hundred dollars for two hours easy work. I thought I owed him a little posthumous consideration.

'I'll take you there,' I said. 'Unexplained client death is bad for business.'

Frank said okay, put my hundred bucks away in his pocket and we went downstairs.

I thought about the pub Scholfield and I had stopped at on our way to Hunters Hill, but I didn't mention it to Frank; he wasn't likely to tell me what his boss had said to him about the case or the other leads they might be pursuing, so why should I flap my mouth? The police driver drove like they all do, as if the roads were built for them alone. We made good time to Hunters Hill. The house was a big, white-painted place, almost showy with its lush garden and the ironwork picked out in black on the gates and the driveway being just long enough to have a small, prestigious, bend in it.

We sat in the car and looked at the house.

'You sure he went in?' Frank said. 'He didn't just hide in the bushes for a while?'

'He went in, stayed half an hour, maybe less, came out. I waited out here. He took a bag in— lightweight, zippered thing—and came out with his hands in his pockets.'

'What then?'

'We were in my car. I drove him back to town. Dropped him in Broadway.'

Frank snorted. 'You must've had a peg on your nose the whole time. You didn't see anyone in the house?'

I shook my head.

'Eloquent. Okay, let's take a look.'

The three of us got out of the car, crossed the

street and didn't bother trying to look inconspicuous. It was an unusual experience for me—pushing open a gate and marching up to a front door without having to think about pretending to be someone else or how to prevent the door being slammed in my face. I tried to enjoy it, but somehow it didn't seem to be as much fun.

Frank rang the bell until the chimes inside got boring. Back off the porch and down around the side: the lush garden didn't look so lush up close. It *had* been carefully tended in the past but was beginning to look a little dried out at the edges. The back of the house was an extravaganza in glass; double doors were set between ceiling-to-floor windows; cane blinds shaded cork-tiled floors. The driver looked enquiringly at Frank and when he got the nod he pulled out a bunch of keys and started on the lock. I glanced across at the big garage with its double roller-door and heard the lock open before I could look back. None of us pulled his gun; we'd all been inside empty houses before and we were not afraid.

It was a lot of house to be standing empty—four bedrooms, two bathrooms, big modern kitchen and rooms for sitting and eating in. All the relevant activities could've been done there with considerable comfort, but it didn't look as if much of anything had gone on for some time. There was a layer of dust over a lot of the surfaces: a trained observer might have detected more; as for me, I'd say the odd person or two had had a snack and a drink and a wash of the hands lately. The toilet had been used, too. The power and water were on and the phone was connected; there was food in the cupboards and more plus beer and wine in the refrigerator. Like all snoopers, we began by creeping and ended by stamping our feet. We didn't say anything because there was nothing to say. Re-grouped at the back door, we looked to Frank for leadership.

'Let's try the garage,' he said.

'Funny,' I whispered. 'That's what I was going to say.'

The driver looked enquiringly at Frank again; with a different superior he might've got a chance to practise his kung-fu, but Frank was used to me. He closed his eyes and mimed counting to ten. 'Cliff,' he said. 'I wish I could have you on the force, with me out-ranking you, just for a little while.'

We were walking towards the garage. 'What would you do, Frank?'

He stopped and looked back at the house. 'Right now, I'd send you to look up in the roof and down into the foundations.'

'Messy,' I said. 'Let's hope we find the money and the bodies and the confessions in the garage.'

The driver was an artist—the roller-door came up just like it does in the commercials and we stepped into a space big enough to hold three cars and light enough to play table tennis in. But there were no cars and no table tennis table—instead, there were a couple of benches covered with jars and retorts and plumbed for hot and cold water. There were bottles and brushes and magnifying glasses and a microscope. There were powders and pastes, tubes of goo and glass plates with metal clamps. I followed Parker as he ranged along the nearest bench; the biggest bottle had a screw top and Parker spun it off.

'Well?'

'Can't be sure,' he said. 'But I think it's the blue stuff that gets onto the money.'

'You know what that makes this set-up, then?'

'Yeah,' he growled. 'Looks like this is where they try to get it off.'

And that was the way it looked a few days later when a microscopic examination of my hundred dollar note had been made. Frank Parker rang me with the good news.

'Serial number checks with a run stolen from a bank in Parramatta last month. Traces of the dye—not visible to the naked eye. Someone's found a way to take it off.'

'What about my money?'

'Sorry, mate. Evidence.'

'Great. What about the house?'

'Nothing. Clean as a whistle. Leased under a phoney name, paid for in cash.' His laugh was a harsh bark. 'Cash?'

'Don't be bitter. You must have something to go on.'

'Not a bloody thing. Looks like they just cleared out after your pal Scholfield went for the jump.'

'Are you looking for people who've turned blue lately?'

'Have you got any other helpful comments, Cliff?'

'Can't you just take a photo of it?'

'What?'

'My hundred bucks.'

That finished the conversation with Parker and left me wondering what to do next. It wasn't that I didn't have a case on hand; I was on a retainer from a security firm to check on some of their employees who were suspected of not rattling the doors they were supposed to rattle and not shining their torches where and when they were supposed to shine them. It was night work mainly, but not exclusively. I had the job for a month and was only half way through. The company didn't expect a perfect record from its men, apparently that was unheard of; it was a question of 'acceptable levels of non-performance'. I ran over some of the results I'd got so far, but I couldn't keep my mind on the job. I kept getting pictures of Norman Scholfield trying to cope with worry in a good-humoured way. I didn't like the idea of someone throwing him off a twenty-storey building—that was too much for good humour. Then I remembered the pub.

Balmain has lost a lot of its good pubs to the bulldozer and to solicitors who've wanted interesting-looking buildings for their offices in which they can arrange the conveyancing of other interesting buildings. But this one was a survivor, and Scholfield had directed me there with a note in his voice like pride. It was down by the water with a balcony that gave you a good view of the container terminal; but there's something agreeable about drinking while other people work. We had a beer in the sun and he'd borrowed my pen. I saw him ring directory enquiries, scribble on the phone book and then make a quick call. He gave me back the pen—a thick-writing ballpoint with purplish ink.

It was much the same time of day again when I got to the pub and I bought a beer and retraced my steps. The water was still there and the container terminal; the directory was there too and the numbers stood out clearly on the page in thick purple backhand.

I sipped the beer and thought how unprofessional I was being, but then, that's one of the advantages of my non-profession. I dialled the number and heard a heavily accented woman's voice on the line.

'Yes? Yes?'

'Norman Scholfield, please.'

There was a pause and then the voice came through slowly and emotively. 'He is not here. Who is calling, please?'

In this business you make all sorts of half-arsed judgements; I took a punt now that this voice belonged to someone who wasn't glad that Norman had free-fallen without a 'chute. 'I'd rather not say on the phone. I have something that might interest him. Could you ask him to meet me? Are you in touch?'

'Yes. Where should he meet you?'

I named the pub. 'I'll be up on the balcony, he knows the place. We had a drink here a few days ago. I'll have a can of Fosters all ready for him. Umm ... I take it he's just stepped out or something? I would like to see him soon.'

'Yes. An hour?'

'Good. Thank you.'

I went for a walk around the streets, wondering what was going to happen next. It was a mild winter day; the sunshine was fitful and the water turned from a greenish blue to a hard grey in response to it. A small yacht moved along in the choppy water looking incongruous against the backdrop of cargo, machinery and work. Fifty-five minutes later, I was back on the balcony with a fresh beer and a clean glass and a can of Fosters in front of me.

She came in. Dead on time. She was tall, with black hair, olive skin and eyes and a nose like a Coptic mask. She was wearing a camel-coloured coat and boots and as she stood in the doorway there wasn't a man within sight who wasn't staring at her. She walked over to me and sat down and I could feel and hear breaths hissing out between clenched teeth from all around.

'Norman couldn't come,' she said.

'I know. He's dead.' I opened the beer can and poured some into my glass. 'This was his drink, wasn't it?'

'Yes. That was his drink.'

'And who're you? I know you've got a new phone number lately. I'd say Norman was important to you, and you don't look like a relative. I don't know anything else about you.'

'Why did you want to see Norman?' She tramped right over what I'd been saying as if the words were a minor nuisance.

'I didn't, I wanted to see you.'

She made a move to get up but I got my hand across, gripped her arm and pressed her down. 'Wait. Let's talk, what harm can it do? Will you have a drink?'

She subsided and shrugged. In the smooth, brown skin of her face, especially around her eyes, were lines of strain and desperation. Her face looked too strong to ever show unhappiness as we lesser mortals do, but it was there. I got her a gin and tonic, and drank the Fosters while she took a few sips. Her teeth were even and white and she had long. slender hands with pink, polished nails cut short. She had a black turtleneck sweater on under the coat, no jewellery. I told her about my brief association with Scholfield, my scouting about with the cops and then waited for her contribution.

'You didn't give my number to the police?'

I shook my head.

'Why didn't you?'

'I don't know. If he was working with some people at getting dye off stolen money I don't really care. It sounds like a pretty dumb scheme and he didn't look dumb to me. I liked him. I suppose I'm just curious. Do you know who killed him, or why?'

'No. If I did, I would kill them.'

'Perhaps it's just as well then.'

'I don't understand you.' The skin tightened along her exquisite jawline; she was like an arrow in a bow—all lined up with the string tight.

I finished the beer. 'Revenge is old-fashioned.' I muttered. 'Let it go.'

'No! He was a lovely man, so funny. We laughed all the time. I know he was not always honest, not so very honest. But he didn't hurt people, just . . .' She waved her hands and all the men looked at her again.

'Institutions,' I said. Frank had told me that Scholfield's frauds were insurance jobs, mostly.

'So. He was a gentle man. I think the one who killed him should be dead too. I would feel better then.'

'In gaol,' I said. 'We don't kill people anymore for murder, not here.' I don't know why it was, maybe just the idea of her feeling better because her man's killer was out of action got to me. I'd come close to Norman's condition more than once and no one would have given a damn. Not that I'd really want anyone to. It was a confused sort of feeling. She nodded vigorously.

'Gaol. Yes. For a very long time. Will you work for me?'

'Eh?'

'You are a detective. You worked for Norman, you can work for me. I can pay you enough. Find out for me who killed him.'

The proposition rocked me, but maybe it was what I had in mind all along. She told me that she was from the Philippines and had come to Australia as a sort of mail-order bride. She thought her blood was more Indian than Filipino but she wasn't sure. This had happened almost ten years ago, when she was eighteen; she'd put up with six years of near-imprisonment until Scholfield had broken her out. She didn't give me the details and I didn't ask. She and Scholfield had been lovers since then, on an irregular basis because he was often out of town. He'd help set her up in business as a handicrafts dealer. The way she told it, she had immigration and tax problems and Norman had marital problems, but she'd loved him and he was all aces to her.

'Did he tell you what he was doing, I mean ... recently?'

'No. He never told me details. Big, he said. Very big. He treated it as a joke. But I don't think it was a joke. He was very worried when he rang me the last time.'

'Was that ...' I searched my memory and came up with the date. 'And about this time of day?'

'Yes.'

'He *was* worried, I was with him. He was worried two hundred bucks worth.'

'I will pay you ten times that to find who killed him.'

'Put it like that and I'd be glad to. Where would I start? Any ideas Miss ...?'

'Seneka, Louise Seneka. I don't know. I am thinking.'

Just to watch her think was a pleasure. She'd drunk about two-thirds of her drink, but the ice had melted and she'd lost interest in it. I'm a bit that way with a g & t myself, so I tend to slug them down. She didn't smoke or fidget in any other way. She sat and concentrated and you could almost feel the force of the concentration. Scholfield had been a tall, slim man with thick fair hair, cut short. He wasn't handsome but he looked extremely healthy, which almost amounted to the same thing. They'd have made a good, contrasting pair. One thing was sure, with a woman like that to keep company with, he wouldn't have jumped.

'He left something for me to post, in a coat at my place. I didn't do it. After he was dead I didn't want to look.'

'Could be a start,' I said. 'Let's go. How did you get here?'

'A taxi.'

'We'll go in my car then.' We went down the stairs and out onto the street. My car was parked around the corner and I took her arm to steer her; her arm was incredibly slender but felt very strong. I was completely distracted by her physicality; the warmth and the light bones. I was utterly off-guard, and when the man moved from behind the car next to mine and dug the gun into my ribs it took me slow, dumb seconds to react. And that made it too late.

'You and the lady get in the car. You in the front and her in the back. I'll kill him, lady, if you don't get in.'

I propped and she must have felt me go rigid as I gripped her arm. She got the message and went with me as I shuffled towards the black Fairlane. The gunman tapped me to indicate how I should bend and prodded me forward. I went. He was good; his big heavy body dealt with me and blocked her off at the same time. She got into the back with him, and I sat down beside a youngish Asian who started the car and got it moving quickly and smoothly. I felt the gun on my neck.

'You got a gun?'

'No, I don't usually carry one when we go out for a drink.'

'Don't shit me, Hardy. You never met her before. We've been trailing you since Scholfield used you to chauffeur him to Hunters Hill. This is the first interesting thing you've done. That was Norman's favourite pub.'

That made him information-rich as well as gun-rich, a dangerous combination.

'She's a client. What's the idea?'

His voice was level, almost bored. 'The idea is you shut up until we get where we're going.'

'Where's that?' He answered me with a vicious dig of the gun into my neck and I shut up. The Asian drove like an angel; his hands barely moved and he touched the brake pedal as if it was a soap bubble. The car glided back towards the city as the afternoon light died and a little sprinkle of rain settled the dust. The driver left the freeway at Darling Harbour and wound up through the streets that avoid the bridge approaches. It was dark when we stopped in a lane which dead-ended in a high, dark ruin that was overdue for demolition. The gunman hustled us out of the car, and the driver backed out of the lane and took off.

A dead-end and sheer brick walls on either side, there was nothing to do but obey the gun. He shepherded us to a deeply recessed door and ordered me to knock on it. I did and stepped back when bright light hit me as the door opened. A small, dark man in a suit stepped away from the door and the gunman motioned Louise Seneka and me to pass him.

'Any trouble, Willie?' the man in the suit asked.

'None. What's up? Why the suit?'

'Appointment. I've got to go out.'

'You mean you've got no guts for it.'

We were standing on frayed lino tiles in a lobby with an old lift and a badly hung door standing open. Through the door I could see a room with a chair and desk. The whole place had an uncomfortably spare feel to it, but the feeling might have just been a product of the rather strained conversation of our hosts.

'This is a mistake,' I said, just for the sake of saying something.

'You might think so very soon,' Willie said. 'You're staying, Barnes. Let's get them in there and get on with it.'

Barnes took out a handkerchief, which was dirty. It looked strange coming out of the pocket of his clean suit; but then, he didn't look as if he wore a suit all that often. He wiped his sweating, red face and then his hands. 'All right,' he said.

We all trooped through into the office-like room and Willie kicked the door shut behind him. There was a chair in front of the desk and he pushed me down onto it. Barnes pointed to the corner of the room behind the desk.

'Go and sit over there.'

Louise Seneka looked at him. 'On the floor?'

'Yes.'

'What are you going to do?'

No one said anything to that; she walked across and crouched in the corner.

'Right down!' Willie barked. She sat, and looked defiant.

There was no natural light in the room, just harsh fluoresence; I could smell dust in the air, also fear, mostly mine. Barnes went behind the desk and Willie perched on it, about three feet away from me.

'No beating about the bush,' Willie said. 'Norman Scholfield gave you something, you or the woman. It's ours and we want it. Hand it over!'

I glanced across at the woman; she'd opened her coat and I could see her slim body, held straight and tense. Our eyes met and she shook her head.

'Can't help you,' I said. 'Spent two hours with the bloke. He made a delivery, I went along for company. That's it.'

'Maybe the woman's got it,' Barnes said.

Willie got off the desk and went over to the corner.

'Well?'

She shook her head.

'Just like him,' Willie said. 'Nothing to say. Could

be he was protecting you?'

She looked at him with those dark, hooded eyes and if he could see anything in them except hate and defiance he was sharper than me.

'Looks like it.' Willie put his foot on her bent knee and pressed down. She gasped sharply but kept looking straight at him. Willie smiled and moved his foot. He stepped back and circled around behind me.

'Put your hands behind you, 'round the chair.' He clipped me lightly on the back of the head with the gun as he spoke and I did what he said. I felt something rough bite into my wrists; I resisted, but with a couple of jerks and a steadying touch with the gun he had my hands tied.

'Okay,' Willie said. 'Last chance. Anything to say?'

My shirt was wet by now and I could feel my scrotum tightening and a nerve dancing in my face. I shook my head.

'Barnes.' The small man loosened his tie and pulled his collar open. He bent and reached into the back of the desk. What he came up with was a small blowtorch. I watched, fascinated, while he primed and pumped it. The flame shot out, red and yellow, and the torch gave out a low roar. Barnes moved around the desk; he was sweating as much as me, but what really sliced into my consciousness now was that he liked it. He fought against it—probably every time—but come right down to it, this was his jollies. It was a nasty sight—the roaring torch, Barnes's rictus of a smile and his running nose. I could feel the heat of the flame and I thought desperately for something to throw them, anything. Nothing came.

I heard Louise scream as Barnes brought the jet close to my ankles, but he was past hearing anything. The flame seared into my stretched skin and seemed to cut to the bone. I felt, rather than heard, my bellow and strength flooded into me, brimming me full. I lashed out with my feet and the torch and Barnes went flying back; I reared up and whipped around, carrying the chair with me. The back fell apart and I rushed at Willie before he could get his gun up. I hit him with everything at once—head, foot, shoulder; I threw my body at him like a missile and hurtled him back into the wall. He hit it awkwardly and hard and the breath went out of him in a rush. I stumbled and fell to my knees—both knees hammered down into Willie's chest with my full weight.

It seemed like minutes before I could force myself back up. I heard the torch roaring softly and when the mist had cleared from my eyes, I saw Barnes lying on the ground, still and twisted. The jet of flame was playing on his outstretched hand, but he didn't move. I went over, hobbling, and eased the torch away with my foot. My hands had been tied to the struts of the chair and there was some slack in the cord; I used the flame to cut through it. One side of Barnes's face was a red-black mess; one eye was obliterated, the other was open and still.

Louise Seneka stood with her back to the wall. She looked like a bronze statue—a statue with a gun in its hand. The gun was pointed at Willie.

'It's all right,' I gasped. 'Don't shoot him.' I moved towards her and she swung the gun on me.

'Stop there! I know about guns. Do what I say or I will wound you and kill him. Is the small one dead?'

'I'd say so, yes.'

'Good! Animal, both animals!'

'Sure. Let's get the police.'

'No, not police. I must know why Norman was killed.'

'We'll find that out from Willie.'

Willie had recovered his breath—almost—and had propped himself up against the wall. He was cradling his shoulder and his pale, fleshy face was chalky white. There was red spittle around his mouth, but he didn't look close to tears. His eyes were on the gun. The woman saw it and smiled.

'He thinks I won't shoot him. He doesn't know about the Philippines. I have seen many people shot; I have seen my brothers shot and I have shot two men myself.'

'I believe you,' I said. 'But we don't want any shooting here. This one's not a big fish, he'll talk to save his own skin. We'll find out what happened.'

'No! He will have reasons not to talk. There will be lawyers and much time wasted. I want to know *now*! Get up!'

Willie could see she meant it; he hoisted himself up, still supporting one arm.

'Shoulder's broken,' he said.

The blowtorch sputtered, coughed and the flame died. We all looked at it. The woman gestured with the gun.

'Go out to the lift.'

We went out into the lobby and I pressed the button to call the lift. My ankles were screaming where the flame had touched them, but I could walk; standing still was harder. I leaned against the wall while we waited for the lift in the silent building. It came. She herded us in and pressed the button for the top floor, the eighth. The lift was old and creaky and slow. As we passed the floors it looked more and more as if the building was unoccupied.

The top floor was stripped clean; it was bare boards and peeling walls. There were large windows along one wall with some of the city night light coming through them, not much. Louise glanced around and saw a heavy swivel chair near the lift.

Willie stood stiffly, watching her, watching me.

'Get over to the window, animal! Hardy, bring the chair.'

The window was an old-fashioned job which had a low, knee-high sill and extended up above head height. She pointed at it.

'Break the bottom part of the window with the chair.'

Willie got the idea a fraction ahead of me. 'No!' he said.

'Break it!'

I slammed the chair into the window frame; the old wood gave and the bottom panes fell through, leaving an empty space for about a metre above the sill.

'Sit there!'

Willie sat on the sill, keeping his feet firmly anchored on the floor and as much of his body inside as he could.

'Move the chair this way, Hardy, and stand by the window—there.'

I did as she said and she sat on the chair, facing Willie and the open gap and about a metre and a half back. She raised the gun.

'Tell me.'

Willie got it out in gulps and gasps: the people he worked for had a double scheme running—counterfeiting, and removing the dye from hot money. The plan was to get both kinds of money into circulation by confusing the authorities. It was all to do with serial numbers and switching denominations—elaborate stuff. Norman had been in on the counterfeiting side of it and had flipped when he'd heard about the other aspect of the deal. He'd wanted out, and tried to get some leverage by nicking one of the counterfeiting plates. The masters said the mess was Barnes and Willie's responsibility and Willie said they were handling it alone.

'Anyone know you picked us up?' I said.

'No. The driver doesn't know who you are.'

'What did Norman tell you about the plate?'

Willie spoke carefully, watching his balance, 'He said something about a coat, that was all. Then he shut up. Wouldn't say a word.'

She looked at me. 'The coat, at my place. He protected me from the animals.' She looked back at Willie. 'So you killed him. You threw him from twenty storeys.'

'It was an accident. I was just trying to scare him.'

She sighed and seemed to relax. 'You tell me, Hardy, that in this country a murderer goes to gaol for a long time.'

'That's right,' I said, but I was thinking—*sometimes*.

She moved up from the chair; Willie leaned in from the sill. She beckoned me close and handed me the gun. I took it. *An automatic, S & W model. 39*, I thought. Willie eased forward and up.

Louise Seneka moved faster than Carl Lewis; she spun the chair and rammed it hard into Willie's midsection; he doubled-up, reeled back and she whipped the chair into him again. He went through the window in a helpless collapse and his scream seemed to flow back in through the gap and fill the room.

I rubbed my sleeve over the chair and the lift buttons; she didn't even look into the room at the bottom and I didn't go in. We hadn't touched anything in there. We were out of the building and had covered a couple of couple of blocks before the sirens started. She didn't speak in the taxi and neither did I. We collected my car in Balmain and drove to her flat in Bellevue Hill, still with the minimum of speech.

The flat was big and light and had just enough east Asian decoration to be interesting. She opened a closet and took out a heavy tweed overcoat on a hanger. From an inside pocket she pulled out a flat, brown paper-wrapped package about the size of a video cassette. She handed it to me. A post office box number and address was printed boldly on the brown paper.

'You think I was wrong?'

'You said taking revenge would make you feel better—did it?'

As I spoke, my eye fell on a bright poster on the wall; the burst of colour reminded me of the blowtorch flame and I went cold inside. She considered my question.

'Yes,' she said.

'Good.'

'You need treatment for your legs.'

I looked down; from the instant Willie had gone out the window until that moment, the burn hadn't hurt. I saw that the synthetic material of my socks had singed and hardened, and was sticking to the raw, burnt flesh. It hurt like hell.

'I know a doctor, better get to him.'

'I would like to pay the expense, also for your help, Mr Hardy. Thank you.'

She held out her hand and I shook it. Her skin was warm, and there was the same strength in her hand that I'd felt in her arm. She was strong all over and inside as well. *She's the most beautiful thing in the world*, I thought, and then I realised that the pain was making me dopey.

'Okay, Miss Seneka,' I said. 'I'll send you a bill.'

I headed for home, wincing every time I had to use the clutch and brake. At home I could phone my medical mate, Ian Sangster, who'd come over and dress my wounds and prescribe some pills I could take with alcohol. Before I got there, though, I stopped at the end of Glebe Point Road, hobbled to the rail and threw the parcel and the S&W.39 as far as I could out into the dark water.

P. I. Blues

Nothing was going right; I hadn't had a client in two weeks and I hadn't paid a bill for a month. That's the way you have to look at it in this game—it's clients balanced against bills. If it ever gets to be clients balanced against bank account I won't know what to do. My ex-wife, Cyn, once told me that I was a private investigator because I didn't have the character to starve in a garret. Maybe she was right; anyway she didn't stick around to starve with me and make it romantic.

My mind was running on romance when the phone rang—maybe this was it.

'Hardy Investigations.' I realised I was crooning like Kamahl. 'Hardy speaking,' I said gruffly.

'You sound like two different people.' The voice was young, female and educated, a winning combination for someone who is more or less the opposite.

'Not really, I was thinking about two different things at once. I can do that sometimes. How can I help you, Ms ...?'

'You can help me by thinking about just one thing—how I can get my ex-husband to pay me the two hundred thousand dollars he owes me.'

'It sounds well worth thinking about,' I said.

'She said you'd be interested. She also said you were good at your work.'

'She being?'

'Kay Fletcher.'

'Aha.'

'She said you'd say that too. I've got a letter from her for you.'

'Did she tell you what I'd say to that?'

'No. She didn't know. Will you see me?'

Kay Fletcher was a journalist I'd had a brief affair with a few years before. She was based in Canberra then and had moved on and up to New York since. We'd clicked well at first, and then her ambition and my inertia pulled us apart. I'd thought of her often but had not made contact beyond a letter and a card.

My caller's name was Pauline Angel, and I asked her to come round to my office from her hotel in Double Bay. That gave me time for a quick shave and brush up, and a clearing of the rubbish off the desk and a general rough dusting with a copy of *Newsweek*.

She was everything her voice had promised; there was New York stamped on her clothes and the city had brushed her Australian voice a bit. I put her age at around thirty, which would have made her a few years younger than Kay and a few more still younger than me. Her class was middle, her intelligence was upper. She handed me the envelope and I put it away in a drawer.

'Aren't you going to read it?'

'Not until I'm wearing my silk pyjamas.'

'I'm not sure I like that remark; it's cheap.'

'You don't have to like it. I'd be embarrassed to read the letter in front of you—I might laugh or cry. Tell me about the two hundred thousand.'

'Ben and I split up a year ago, in New York actually. We had an apartment near the park and we sold it—Ben sold it, but it was in both names. I signed the papers. Just over four hundred thousand dollars. Jesus!' She got a cigarette out of her jacket pocket and lit it. I passed an ashtray across and tried to concentrate on the two hundred grand rather than a few cents worth of cigarette smoke. I didn't find it easy.

'You're legally divorced?'

'Sure. Ben's married again. But we didn't make any legal arrangements about a settlement or anything—it was just understood that the money'd be split fifty-fifty.

'No two people understand the same when it comes to money. He won't divvy?'

'He says it's all gone. I don't believe him.'

'Gone how?'

'In a shares deal; it's absurd, he's an architect, he doesn't know about shares.'

I could have told her about some people who didn't know about shares until they found out the hard way, but I didn't. In my experience, people who've lost a lot of money usually have a fair bit left. I took some of hers from her, got her address and the details on the husband, and promised her I'd look into it and report quickly. At one hundred and twenty-five dollars per day—that's the least I could do.

It was a nice day for a drive, particularly for a drive to Watsons Bay. The address Ms Angel had given me turned out to be for a house overlooking Camp Cove and therefore the city and other expensive and expansive views. I stood outside it for a minute, looking down past the house at the view—that was free and no-one tried to stop me.

That all changed when I reached the gate which was a high, solid, metal-bound piece of hardware set on massive hinges in a wall that looked thick enough to withstand artillery. I banged with the heavy knocker and heard a bell ring inside—nice trick. Then I noticed a bell button on the wall and I pressed it, but it only got me more bell, not knocking. I felt disappointed, and was ready to be critical when I heard footsteps approaching the gate. Heavy footsteps, big-man footsteps. The face that appeared when the well-concealed panel in the gate lifted wasn't one you'd make suggestions to about the doorbell. The face was big and broad to start with, and ugly to go on with—heavy, dark brows under a crew cut and everything underneath, the broken nose, scarred eyes and thin, battered mouth saying *TOUCH*.

'Yes sir?' The 'sir' came out strangled, as if it was a word in a foreign language he'd just recently learned.

'Is this Mr Angel's residence?'

'Yes.' His hands, well out of sight, moved quickly; he brought a camera up to the aperture in the gate and quickly snapped my picture. Probably not one of my best with my mouth hanging open. 'What d'you want?' he rumbled.

'Never mind.' I ducked aside and walked off, feeling like idiot of the month.

It was late afternoon, time to drive my humiliation home with me to Glebe and give it a drink and do some thinking. As it turned out I didn't get the chance to drink or think; I walked up the overgrown path to my terrace house and the house fell on me; then the ground turned to thin air and all sights and sounds turned into a roaring black hum.

When I came out of it I was lying on my back in the passageway inside the house. The peeling wallpaper and tattered carpet isn't too good at the best of times, and wasn't nice to regain consciousness with. Neither was the man who stood with his back to the door looking down at me. He looked about eight feet tall but that could have been because I felt about three feet at most myself. He could have been the cousin of the guy at the gate in Camp Cove; he wasn't quite as dark and ugly, but definitely was of the same stamp. He was a bit more articulate.

'I don't know why you paid us a visit this afternoon, Hardy, and I don't want to know. Some mistake, I assume. We don't want trouble and I'm sure you don't want trouble. Am I right?'

'Don't want trouble,' I said dumbly.

'Good. That's all there is for you if you go out there again—or if you write or phone or interfere in Mr Angel's affairs in any way. Clear?'

'Mud,' I said.

'Don't try to be smart, you're not smart. He stepped closer and tapped the side of my head with his shoe.' Be careful, or you'll end up even dumber than you are now. I'll say it again—clear?'

I nodded, and felt a momentary return of the black hum.

'Good, I hope we don't ever have to meet again.' He opened and closed the door in a fluid motion, and I lay on the carpet for a while trying to think of all the things I knew that other people didn't know so I could check that my brain and personality were undamaged. It didn't take long and it didn't make me feel good. I got up and staggered first to the bathroom and then, with a wet, towel-draped head, to the kitchen. I drank some wine, and it tasted like turpentine so I had to go quickly back to the bathroom again. The second time the wine stayed down, and even began to taste quite good by the third glass.

Sitting there aching and getting drunk, my mind naturally began to run on failure. I tried to think of the cases I'd abandoned for one reason or another. There were a few, given up because I'd been lied to in the first place or because the trouble I was looking into had happened too long ago. I could only think of one given up because I'd been scared, and then I was scared of the police and the politicians and only someone with concrete brains wouldn't have been scared. I was scared now and I didn't like it. Emptying my pockets to get into a more comfortable drinking posture, I turned up Kay's letter. I smoothed it out, poured more wine, and read it.

Dear Cliff,
I've thought of you often, wondering how you were and whether you've had any regrets about us. I got your letter, but it didn't say much and I was gung ho after some story or other at the time.
I've calmed down a bit and I'm considering an offer from a Sydney paper. Good offer and Sydney's the only place in Australia I'd want to work. Don't know what you feel about me but I'd love to see you again. Don't feel threatened for Chrissake—just telling you I'm thinking of coming back and I've got no ties.
I hope you can help my friend Pauline who's a peach who made the bad mistake of marrying a lying shit. She's worth helping, Cliff; I did a bit when she made the break but she needs brains and guts now on the money matter, and that's you in my book. If you can get the money for her I'll be confirmed in my feeling that you're a prince.
See you soon, I hope.
love,
KAY

It made me think of the few nights I'd spent with Kay and the many nights I'd spent without anyone, and I wanted to see her very badly. My head started to hurt less and I started to feel angry—maybe it was my pride coming back. I had a few days worth of Pauline Angel's money and an incentive—more than enough motivation. I drank some coffee, showered, put some healing ointment on my head and a cap over it, and went back to work.

A few phone calls deepened the mystery—Ben Angel was an architect all right, but he didn't seem to do much business. He was an American who'd acquired right of residence on Australia through his marriage to Pauline. He'd opened an office in Sydney and there was talk of big contracts, but so far it was just talk. I couldn't get anything about his career in America at such short notice except the suggestion that his name might originally have had a few more vowels and consonants in it. Mrs Angel II was more accessible—she worked at a TV station as a PR person. My informant was a journalist who happened to know that Tolley Angel was hosting a small party at the station that evening.

'Tolley?' I said.

'That's the name she goes by.'

'How would I spot her?'

'Look up, they tell me she's six foot two.'

I drank some more coffee and went out wearing my cap and poplin raincoat and trying to look French. The TV station was on the north side, and I drove into the parking area as if I belonged.

There weren't many of the minions cars around but the executives' spaces were pretty well filled with Mercs, Volvos and the like. I tried to guess which of the cars would be Tolley Angel's; and had settled on a black Porsche when she came out of the building—that is, a six-foot-two brunette with an executive briefcase and about a thousand dollars worth of clothes on her back came out. She seemed to be in a hurry, because she almost ran to a silver grey BMW and took off with spinning wheels and spitting gravel. I followed her, blowing smoke.

The BMW wound down through Lane Cove towards the city. It wasn't hard to follow because she drove well, signalling early and making her moves decisively; it was a pleasure to watch her drive. She stopped in Drummoyne in a street that didn't have anything in particular to recommend it and when I saw a middle-aged man in fashionable casual clothes come bouncing out of an ordinary looking house, jump the low fence and grab her as soon as she got clear of the car, I was so surprised I nearly leaned on the horn. They hugged and kissed enthusiastically, and then he escorted her back into the house with his arm around her so tightly she could hardly walk. She wasn't protesting. I was parked a few cars away; the light was poor but the film in the camera was fast. I got the whole show, frame by frame. After a scarcely decent interval she came out of the house, alone; the front of her dress was unbuttoned in manner not dictated by fashion and her hair had escaped its modish arrangement and was hanging loose. She reached into the car and pulled out a wrapped bottle: I snapped her—dress, hair, bottle and all—and felt like the second-assistant pimp.

She went back into the house, happy and jaunty and somehow I didn't think she'd be out soon. I didn't feel like hanging around to see if she did up her dress right or what the brand of the wine was; I drove home and started on some wine of my own. My head was hurting and not only from the earlier beating; I had one of my periods of self-dislike at what I did for a living. I believed in people doing what made them feel good and I didn't like fingering them because other people didn't like them doing it. There's no remedy except to grow another skin and push on. I used the Council rate roll to identify Tolley Angel's lover—Claude Murray and the telephone book gave me his trade—screenwriter. Call it prejudice, but the hyphen made me feel just a little better. I took a glass of wine and a biography of Scott Fitzgerald to bed. I read for a little while, thought about Kay and then I slept.

Pauline Angel was living in a friend's house in Balmoral close to the beach and not too close to the neighbours. The house was set on a bigger block of land than is usual in those parts, and the grass and the white paint and the palm trees on either side and in front gave it a feel of the Raj, which would be pretty easy to take in most moods. I went up the steep path in front to the wooden steps that led to a high verandah, running the width of the house. The air felt cleaner just those few metres up. I'd phoned, she was expecting me and there was a pot of tea and milk and mugs on a table in the open. I accepted the tea and repressed the shudder.

She was going to have to nice tan soon, but the strain in her face was beginning to eat at her good looks.

'Nice place,' I said. 'Your husband has a pretty nice place too.'

'Ex-husband. Has he? I've never been there.'

'Yeah, it's got better security than this—high wall, peep hole, bodyguard ...'

'You're joking!'

'I'm not.' I lifted the cap and fingered the back of my head which was tender; a little blood came off on my hand and I showed it to her. 'One of the bodyguards paid me a visit. He warned me off with a blunt instrument.'

'I don't understand.'

'Neither do I. Mrs Angel, you told me your husband was an architect. I've met the odd architect but I never met one who employed muscle. How well did you know him? How long were you married?'

She drank some tea, and looked out across the palm tops to the water like a castaway hoping to see a sail. 'We were married for four years, he was away a lot. He travelled all over the States on business. He did work for all kinds of big companies. He didn't talk about it much. I was busy too; I was studying at City College.' She pulled a self-mocking face. 'I was studying ceramics, God knows why. Do you know New York?'

'I've been there—wouldn't say I know it.'

'Well, you know what a crazy place it is. It was all foreign to me and Ben was born there, he seemed to know it so well. I didn't know how marriages worked there, he told me ours was fine and I believed him. That sounds crazy doesn't it?'

'Not really. It sounds like New York, though.'

'The truth is I didn't know him very well. No, I didn't know him at all.'

'Kay says he was a liar, what's that mean?'

'In the end I found out he had another woman living in an apartment just like the one we were in, and not far away. I don't think he was travelling as much as he said he was.' She finished her tea and lit a cigarette. 'Maybe he never travelled at all, or just across a couple of blocks. I don't know. I loved him, he was great fun. I just can't understand what happened, why he went ... so strange about the money.'

'The place I saw was a half-million dollar job, would you expect him to have that sort of money?'

'No, but I don't know what he's been doing for nearly a year now. He could have made a lot, but why not give me my due?'

'That's the question. Could it have anything to do with his new wife?'

She shrugged and stubbed her cigarette out; it wasn't her favourite topic. 'I don't know. All I know about her is that she's good-looking and she's got a silly name.'

I grunted and she made an effort to jolt her out of her absorption in her problems.

'I'm sorry you were hurt,' she said. 'Kay said you were very tough.'

I smiled. 'I am.'

'She said you were nice, too. She's very fond of you. You haven't drunk your tea.'

I got up from the wicker chair that had been cutting into me. 'She should have told you I hated tea. You've said a lot of interesting things, Pauline. I'm beginning to get a picture of Mr Angel. I'll be getting back to work.'

'Be careful.'

'I will. Kay says she's coming back to look Sydney over soon.'

She smiled the smile that would look so good without the strain. 'Yes, won't it be great to see her?'

'Great,' I said.

That pleasant thought made me sloppy. I ambled back down the path and strolled to my car, mentally rehearsing what I'd say to Kay. I put the key in the lock and suddenly there he was, looking at me from the other side of the car; also looking was the business end of an automatic pistol.

'You don't listen, Hardy,' he said. 'Looks like you'll have to be shown what to do.' His dark eyebrows almost met across the top of his face as he crinkled his eyes in the bright sun. He looked like a gorilla, but the gun made him the zoo keeper.

'Leave this bomb where it is. You're going for a ride in a real car. Move!'

He gestured at a black Fairlane on the other side of the road. The man sitting at the wheel had his gun pointed at my spine.

'Bags I drive,' I said.

Being driven to Camp Cove by that pair was no fun. Ugly I did the driving while Ugly II held his pistol so that if it went off I'd have a big hole in an inconvenient place. The Fairlane cruised slowly past the high front wall, sidled around the side of the house and went through a magic-eye-opened gate into a courtyard big enough to hold it and a couple more. Ugly II prodded me with the pistol and we went up some steps and through some glass and walked across some carpet. It was like wading knee deep through money. My escort tapped on a door and we waited. Inside a telephone was put down and a match was struck, then a deep voice said 'Come in' and we did.

He was sitting behind a big desk smoking a small cigar, but there was nothing corny about him. He was very dark with a heavy beard and his teeth shone whitely in all that swarthiness. He was around forty and looked to be about medium sized but with a lot of power in his shoulders and jaw. The shirt and vest he wore went with the house and his haircut and his manicure and everything about him. Even the cigar smelled good.

'I'm Ben Angel.'

'Congratulations,' I said.

'I'll hire you when I need a comedian. You come here, you go to see my ex-wife, why?'

'Say please and I might tell you.'

I heard Ugly II make ugly noises behind me but I didn't turn round. The body's one big vulnerable place if you know your business, and he did.

'I'll humour you—please.'

He smiled when he said it and I rather wished he hadn't; Ben Angel didn't have to work too hard at being scary, it was all there in the soft voice and the way he kept his hands still.

'Your wife hired me to get you to pay her the two hundred and fifty thousand you owe her.' I thought I might as well up the ante a little. He smiled again.

'Thought it might be that. I thought Joel here could persuade you to leave it be. Didn't work, huh?'

I shook my head.

'Why? You don't look dumb.'

'Reasons,' I said.'

He leaned back in his chair, and seemed to notice for the first time that I was standing up.

'Take a seat, Hardy. Joel, be a nice guy and get us both a drink and stop looming like that. We've got us a reasonable man here, right, Hardy?'

I pulled a stylish metal and fabric chair closer to the desk and sat down, but I didn't admit to being reasonable. Joel handed me a glass and put one just the same on Angel's desk.

'Go check the teleprinter, Joel, Hardy and me are going to have a chat.'

Joel went out quietly and I took a quiet sip of the drink, which was good Scotch with not too much water. Angel had a drink and leaned forward on his desk so that our faces were only six feet apart.

'Here's the thing, Hardy. Pauline thought I was an architect, but I'm not; leastways I was, but . . .'

'Not for long.'

'You've got it—not much and not for long. I've got other interests, a bit of this and a bit of that. Do I make myself clear?'

'The front gate and Joel's .45 help to make the point.' I said.

'Right, now I had a bit of trouble getting into the country with my assets intact and all that. It took a lot of oil in the right places. It's okay but it's delicate. I have to watch my ass. Now, suppose I give Pauline the quarter million, she's so straight what's the first thing she'll do?'

'Clear it with the tax people, after she pays me my fee I hope.'

'Right, so then I have to account for the money and what do I say?'

'Legitimate capital gains on property sold in the US.'

'I didn't sell any apartment in New York, that was just a story for Pauline. I didn't own the apartment. I'm supposed to be clean; a floating two hundred and fifty grand makes me look very dirty. You see my problem?'

I drank some more of the Scotch and saw the problem very clearly, except that I saw it as Pauline's problem and my problem too. 'When can she expect something then? You don't have to keep this cleanskin pose up for ever, do you?'

He opened his hands expressively, the first flourish he'd permitted himself. I noticed then that he had a big stoned, un-architect-like ring on his right hand as well as a broad wedding ring on the left. 'You read the papers—commissions of enquiry into this, investigations of that. It's heads-down time. I can raise the money all right, no problem there, but Pauline's the original Miss Clean. This case, she's her own worst enemy.'

His matey tone and the good Scotch made me incautious. 'What's the new Mrs Angel think about it all?'

He clenched his hand around the glass. 'Have you been snooping around her too? Now that I really don't like.' The matiness was all gone. 'Tell me what you did?'

I finished the drink. 'Nothing.'

'Joel!'

Joel came back into the room and I stood up with the empty glass in my hand and backed towards a wall.

'Our friend here's got some more talking to do, Joel; persuade him.'

He came at me fast and bent low in a crouch which still put his head on a level with my shoulder. I stepped aside and hooked at the head but it wasn't where it'd been a split second before. He slammed me with his left as he moved past and I'd have sworn he landed on exactly the spot he'd hit before. The pain cooled me down for some reason and made me quicker; I walked through a punch and got in close enough to land a short right well below the belt. He wasn't ready for it and he gasped and faltered; I put my knee in the same place and when his head came down I uppercut him with a double clenched fist. He fell away from me, flailed and ripped the front out of my shirt with his clutching hand. Something flew out of the pocket and bounced on Angel's desk. I was breathing hard when I turned to face him and for the second time in two hours I found myself looking into a gun.

'Thought you wanted to stay clean, Angel,' I panted.

'I do. There's a hell of a difference between killing a guy and tax evasion; killing's safer or hadn't you heard?'

'Yeah, I heard. Don't count on it, it was the killing they got Terry Clarke for.' I moved towards the desk. 'I don't think you'd do it.'

He fired and I felt the heat of the bullet as it went past my ear. The door slammed open and Ugly II's face appeared with an expression on it that suggested he was ready to fire bomb the room if he was asked to. Angel waved him away.

'Shoulder, left arm, right arm; you name it, Hardy. What's this?' His hand closed over the roll of film.

'Bugger it all,' I said. I slumped back down into

my chair and looked at Joel who was stirring and muttering darkly. 'What about another drink?'

Angel watched Joel get up and struggle to pull himself together, then he tossed him the film.

'See if you can do a better job with this. Run it down to one of those one hour places. Nothing dirty is there, Hardy? Oh, Joel, before you go you could pour us both another drink.'

We got the drinks and Joel went out. Angel put his gun down on the desk and demonstrated to me how quickly he could pick it up again.

'I can strip it in seventy-four seconds,' he said.

'Let's see.'

He smiled. 'Wouldn't do you any good, there's three other guys in the house as good as me.'

'Better than Joel?'

'Bit of a disappointment, I must admit. Where'd you learn to handle yourself—the service?'

'Partly, Malaya.'

'Yeah? I was in Nam—just for a bit, got too goddamn hot.'

'Private Angel?'

'Sergeant Pietangeli.'

We didn't say much after that and Joel got back with the prints in just over the hour. Angel motioned him away, and let the prints slip out onto the desk. I stopped breathing while he arranged them in a line; he shuffled them around a bit, but the expression on his face told me nothing except that he was interested. He looked up at me and the stillness was back in his eyes and hands.

'Guy's name?'

'Don't know.'

He drained the few drops left in his glass and stared at the wall behind where I was sitting; I'd already looked at it, the bullet had cracked and split the plaster and knocked a chunk out that was roughly the shape of Italy.

'Tell Pauline to be patient.'

'What?'

'Tell her wait. Tell her to borrow some money or something. End of the year at the latest, I'll give her everything she wants. Now, get your lousy Australian ass out of here.'

Kay delayed looking over Sydney several times and it was into the New Year before we were having that first, tentative drink at the airport. She looked wonderful—tall, tanned from skiing and slim from her energetic, self-denying lifestyle.

'You don't look too bad, Cliff, considering.'

'Considering what?'

'You know. When did you last take a break. fishing?'

'Never caught a fish in my life. Boring.'

'Well, Pauline thinks you're the best. She got her money not long after she went to Melbourne.'

'Yeah, she got it.'

'Why so sour about it?'

I hadn't meant to tell her but I did. I gave Pauline Ben Angel's message and she took it to heart—borrowed some money, paid me and went to Melbourne. I didn't feel good about it; the case felt incomplete and although there'd been something totally convincing about Angel I was left with no ideas. Then, a few weeks later, Tolley Angel was killed in a car accident. Along with her was Claude Murray-Jones, forty-nine, screenwriter of Drummoyne. The BMW had left the highway at speed, rolled and burned. The police had asked the driver of another car reportedly at the scene of the accident to contact them, but with no result.

'That's awful,' Kay said. 'But I can't see what is has to do . . .'

'I took some photos of her and this Wilcox. Angel saw them—that was the first he knew they were having an affair. I tipped him off, by accident.'

'Yes.'

'Angel couldn't get his hands on any money he couldn't account for, remember?'

'Yes, Pauline wrote me.'

'There was a three hundred thousand dollar insurance policy on her life. Angel was the beneficiary. That's where Pauline got her money.'

I had another drink and Kay didn't, and it got worse from there. We gave it a try, went to the places you go to when you're trying to be happy, but it didn't work. She didn't like the sound of the job they offered her, she didn't like the editor and she didn't like the weather. I drove her past Angel's place at Camp Cove; she looked but she didn't say anything. Next day she caught a plane back to New York City.

The Arms of the Law

The voice on the phone was hoarse and not much more than a whisper. 'Hardy? This is Harvey Salmon.'

'Oh yeah,' I said, 'and who else?'

'Huh?'

'The way I hear it, Harvey, you haven't had a private phone conversation in years.'

'Don't joke, Hardy. This is serious.'

'Must be. When did you get out?'

'Today. I need your help.'

'Mr Salmon, I'd reckon you need prayers and airline tickets in about that order.'

'Stop pissing around. I want to meet you to talk business. D'you know the Sportsman Club, in Alexandria?'

I did know it although I didn't particularly want to; it was a dive that went back to six o'clock closing days and beyond as a sly grog joint and SP hangout. In those days the sport most of its associates were familiar with was two-up. I'd heard that it had gained some sort of affiliation with a soccer club, but it had still worn the same dingy, guilty look when I last drove past.

'It's one of my favourite places.' I said. 'Are you a member there?'

'Yeah, about the only place I still am a member.' His voice was bitter. 'Meet me there in an hour and we'll talk work and money.'

'I don't know ...'

'A thousand bucks, Hardy, for two days' work.'

'Okay.' The phone clicked as soon as I had the second syllable out. I sat there with the instrument in my hand thinking that I was about to associate with a known criminal. But then, as a private investigator, I did that a lot of the time and it was what my mother had predicted I'd end up doing anyway. Besides, we're associating with criminals all the time—motor mechanics, doctors, real estate agents—it was only the 'known' part that made this any different.

I needed the thousand bucks, not because business was especially slow. It wasn't; I had a few party-mindings and money-escortings to do in the days ahead, and I was on a retainer from a group of wealthy Ultimo squatters who were trying to keep leverage on the smelly company that owned their row of terraces. But things kept getting more expensive, like food and Scotch and sneakers, and it would take a lot of fear to turn me away from a thousand dollars.

The name Harvey Salmon generated a certain amount of fear, mind you. He'd been a key man in a syndicate which the press had dubbed 'the rainforest ring' because the marijuana grown in Australia, or some of it, had been cultivated in rainforests. But the ring had operated on a broad field, importing from South-East Asia and exporting to the US, and there had been the usual number of couriers killed and businessmen who'd found it expedient to go off into the bush with just their Mercedes and a shotgun.

The ring had collapsed under two simultaneous blows—the death, from a heart attack at the age of 43 while jogging, of Peter 'Pilot' Wrench who'd been the chief organiser. Some said that Wrench had got his nickname from his early days of flying drugs into Australia through the open northern door, others said it was really 'Pilate' because he always washed his hands of a bad deal and a bad dealer. The death of Wrench threw the lieutenants into confusion and doubt. One of them gave interviews to certain law enforcement officers which resolved the doubts of some of the others who got long sentences to repent in. The interviewee was Harvey Salmon who'd backed up his allegations with scores of hours of telephone tapes. I'd heard a lot of that on the QT from Harry Tickener and other journalists; for public consumption, Salmon had got fifteen years a mere eighteen months ago.

It was 3 p.m. on a Wednesday afternoon, traffic in Alexandria was light and that made it a halcyon time of day. Alexandria seems to live on hope; the city and airport bound traffic moves through its broad and narrow streets like a cancer, but the area has been promised a park, a big project park. Acres of industrial land, including a bricking quarry and factory, have been slated for development as a park to rival Centennial. People were hanging on to their slum terraces and the real-estate operators were waiting for the park like a kidney patient waits for a donor. Meanwhile, the place is home to a few different ethnic groups and some restaurants to match—most of the restaurants will survive the park, most of the people won't.

I parked only three blocks away from the Sportsman Club, almost back into Erskineville, but that's nearby parking in Alexandria. At 3.30 the club already had a quota of drinkers—some of them afternoon specialists, some for whom the morning session had dragged on a bit, some for whom the evening had started early. I had to wait by a fly-blown receptionist booth while my name was sent 'upstairs'. After I'd spent 10 minutes comparing the fly spots on the glass of the booth to the blackheads on the nose of the girl inside it, Harvey Salmon came down the stairs to escort me into the precincts.

Salmon was tall and heavy with thinning brown hair and an expression that suggested things were bad and getting worse. I'd never met him but his picture had been in the papers at the time of 'Pilot' Wrench's departure; in the flesh he looked heavier, thinner on top and even less sanguine. But gaol changes a man. He stopped a couple of steps from the bottom and studied me carefully. He wore a pale grey suit, white shirt and dark tie, suede shoes; I had on sneakers and jeans, an open-neck shirt and a leather jacket. I wondered which of us was dressed right. Salmon hopped down the last couple of steps with fair agility, gave me a nod and put two dollars between the sliding glass panels of the booth.

'Thanks, Teresa.'

Teresa didn't even glance up from *TV Week*. ''kay,' she said.

I went up the short flight of stairs with Salmon, through a smaller drinking room with fewer poker machines than the one below, and into an office that was dark and musty. The only light was struggling in through some venetian blinds and the only places to sit were on the desk or on a rickety chair behind it. I sat on the desk and Salmon moved towards the chair. He also cleared his throat to speak but I got in first.

'How about a drink?'

'What? Oh yeah, sure, sorry.' He moved back and opened the door; for a minute I thought he was going to yell his order across to the bar but he didn't. He went out and I had about a minute and a half to study the room before he came back with two schooners. A minute and a half was plenty and I hadn't drunk schooners of old for years. It wasn't

43

such a good start.

When he was settled behind the desk and his glass, Salmon cracked his knuckles—I hoped he wasn't going to do that too often.

'I need someone around for two days.' he said.

'Try downstairs. If you're good company you shouldn't have any trouble.'

'I need someone who can handle a little trouble, if it comes up. Not that it will.'

'You never can tell,' I said. 'Especially in your game.'

He ignored me as if he had a set speech to deliver and was going to do it, no matter what. 'I was all set to fly out today, that was the deal.' He paused, maybe to see if I was shocked. I wasn't. 'But there's been some screw-up over the passport. I've got two days to wait, and I've got enemies.'

'Book into the Hilton, watch TV and wait.'

He ruffled the thin hair which made it look even thinner. 'I don't want to do that. Am I going to do that for the rest of my life? The cops say they're keeping an eye on me and also on certain people. But I don't know. Who can you trust?'

I drank some beer and looked at him; he wasn't sweating and he didn't look afraid, but maybe he just lacked imagination the way he, apparently, lacked a sense of irony.

'Where are you going?' I asked.

'R . . . South America. Same thing, see? The cops say they've squared it over there but I want to get a feel of what it's like. I'll have to get someone over there, but I want to do a few things while I've got these couple of days. Jesus, I've lived here fifty years, I don't want to spend the last two days in a hotel room.'

An appeal based on the pleasure of Sydney will get me every time. Salmon could see he had me and he took a confident gulp of his schooner before giving me the details. He had the use of a flat in Erskineville for the next three nights and expected to catch his plane on Saturday afternoon. He had a few places to visit, a woman to see. He wanted to have a few beers here and there; he wanted to go to the trots and the beach. He wanted me to stay in the flat and tag along with him. He'd give me five hundred now and five hundred on Saturday. I said I'd do it. Truth was, I was getting rather bored with party-minding and money-escorting.

We finished our beers and stood up together—the Sportsman wasn't the kind of place you wanted to stick around.

'Got a gun?' Salmon asked.

'Yeah. Got the money?'

'In the flat. Let's go.'

We left the glasses on the desk and went out of the office and through the bar. A couple of the drinkers looked at us but not with any particular interest that I could detect. Still, it's never too early to start doing a job well. Teresa had got to Wednesday in the *TV Week*; we went past her and out to the street. Salmon looked up and down it nervously.

'Where's your car?'

'Here's where you start living like a free man. It's about half a mile away.'

We walked down Margaret Street which was fairly busy with shoppers and strollers and turned into a quiet side street. Salmon didn't seem furtive but he wasn't introducing himself to people either. I noticed that he had a reasonable tan and not a gaol pallor and I asked him about it.

'I did some gardening.' he said.

'I'm surprised they'd let you grow anything.'

He slowed down and gave me what passed for an amused look; the downward drooping lines of his face squared up a little. 'You'd be surprised what grows inside.' He patted down his wavy hair with a brown hand.

When we got to the car he hesitated.

'What's wrong?'

'What year is it?' he said.

'What does it matter? It goes.'

He got in. 'It goes with the flat anyway.' he muttered.

He directed me through the streets to one of the less grimy parts of Erskineville and we pulled up outside an ugly block of red-brick flats. I remembered that Harvey Salmon's address used to be given as 'of Point Piper' but he approached the building unconcernedly.

'It's not much,' he said. 'Cops reckon it's all they can afford. They reckon they've got a couple of the flats in the block so it's safe. What d'you reckon?'

We went down a narrow concrete path to the back of the block and a narrow set of concrete steps that was flanked by a rickety wrought-iron hand rail. Salmon got a bright shining key out of his pocket and unlocked the door. The flat was one of three with doors giving on to a skimpy walkway: no balconies here, no window boxes even.

Inside, the decor was nondescript, new but not very new, and bought from a catalogue rather than according to anyone's taste. I told Salmon to stay by the door while I checked the rooms: the small kitchen and smaller bathroom were empty, so was the bedroom. There was no one in the toilet. Salmon motioned me into the kitchen with a head movement. Out there he opened the fridge and got out a bottle of Reschs. I shook my head; he opened the bottle, poured a glass and drank it straight off. He poured another.

'The place could be bugged.' he whispered. 'What

d'you reckon?'

That was twice he'd asked me, it was time I reckoned something.

'Let's not talk,' I said. 'I'll look around for bugs. Does the TV work?'

'Think so.'

'I'll watch the tennis. When're you going out?'

'Tonight. Sevenish. Think I'll have a kip.'

I cleared my throat and held out my hand.

'Oh, sure.' He reached into the breast pocket of his jacket and pulled out a wallet. He took out five hundred-dollar notes that looked as if they had plenty of company and handed them to me. I put the money in my jeans, peeled off my jacket and draped it over a chair and turned on the television. John Fitzgerald was serving to John Lloyd, 15-40. Salmon didn't even look at the picture. He scratched under his arm and went into the bedroom. I heard the springs groan as he flopped on the bed. Lloyd was at the net but he hadn't put enough snap into his volley and Fitzgerald lobbed over him: 30-40. I made a couple of cups of instant coffee in the kitchen and slept through a doubles match for an hour. Salmon came out and showered and we were set to go at 6.30. Before we went out the door he handed me twenty dollars.

'Expenses,' he said. 'Petrol, drinks and that.'

'Thanks.' I'd been on the job for about three hours and I hadn't done much that was very different from what I did when I wasn't working—except collect five hundred and twenty dollars.

The first stop was a pub in the Cross where Salmon claimed to know a lot of people but they didn't seem to be around that night. We had a couple of drinks and he scratched up a word or two with a few blokes who didn't seem especially keen to talk to him.

'Just killing time,' he said as we hit the street again. 'This is the real business of the night: Lulu.'

I nodded politely; we were walking along Darlinghurst Road and there was a car cruising a few yards back and I was sure I'd seen one of the window-shoppers earlier in the night.

'You've got your tail.' I said, Salmon shrugged. A street girl wearing an open-weave top through which her nipples protruded and a mini-skirt that showed her meaty thighs, ambled out across the pavement and gave us the word. Salmon shook his head; I examined her closely but I was pretty sure she was the real thing and not policewoman somebody.

'Tarts,' Salmon said. 'Wait'll you see Lulu.'

We went into a strip club opposite the 50-flavours-of-ice-cream shop. Salmon showed a card and twenty dollars to the man inside the door and he took us through the smoke to a table down near the stage. I looked around to check for danger spots but I hardly needed to because the place was exactly like a dozen others I'd been in. Maybe I had been in there, it's hard to tell. There was a bar along one wall, maybe twenty or thirty tables, with just enough room for the drink waiters to squeeze between, grouped in front of a wide stage. The stage was covered by a black curtain that had trapped smoke and dust and dreams for too many years. Salmon ordered a double Scotch and beer chaser for himself and I settled for a single Scotch. It was cash on the barrelhead, of course, and he paid from that big roll that made me more nervous than anything else I'd seen.

After a while the show started and there's nothing to say about it except that it was slow and third or possibly fourth rate. The girls had dead eyes and their bodies seemed to come to life only spasmodically. Lulu was marginally more interesting than the rest if only because her enormous breasts looked real and when she glimpsed the wildly enthusiastic Salmon across the footlights she smiled with genuine invitation.

'Wasn't she great?' Salmon said. He waved for another drink; a few more and all he could hope to use those great tits for was a pillow.

'Yeah,' I said. 'She seemed to like you too.'

'That's a hell of a woman, Hardy.' His voice had got slow and grave. Oh God, I thought, a slow, grave drunk. They're possibly worse than the fighting ones. At least you can tap the fighters on the nose, mop up the blood and put them to bed. He leaned forward across the table and whispered through the smoke haze and din of people talking loudly and drunkenly. 'Rang 'er up this morning. She's got a place behind here. I'm goin' back there in an hour, want you to keep an eye out.'

'Okay, but you'd better lay off the booze or you'll be wasting your money.'

'No money!' His voice went up suddenly. 'No money!'

'Okay, okay. Take it easy.' Slow and grave and fighting—the very worst kind.

At the appointed time a waiter beckoned to us and we got up and went through a small door at the end of the room beside the stage. The passageway was dark and there were a couple of rooms off it, one of which was framed in bright light. Salmon gave the waiter some money and he went away. Salmon steadied himself against the wall.

'Been a long time,' he said.

'Mmm?' I was trying to see the end of the passage in the dark. 'Need any help?'

'Funny. You just squat down there somewhere and wait for me.' He waved at the blackness ahead and knocked on the door. It opened and Lulu put her sequined breasts out into the passage where they would have prevented over-taking. Up close her skin looked coarse and heavily powdered but she still had the genuine smile.

'Come in, Harvey,' she said. Salmon went in and I felt my way to the end of the passage. It did a right angle bend, went down some steps and ended in a door that led on to a lane. I had a wide choice: the passage, the street or the stairs. Anyone who stands around in the street in the Cross after dark is asking for trouble; the passage was dark and smelled of cheap perfume and sweat. I chose the stairs.

I sat there in the gloom feeling sorry for myself and thinking that this job hadn't turned out to be much more exciting than party-minding. Some very recognisable sounds came from the room a few metres away; at least Harvey was having a good time. I sat there remembering good times and feeling the $505 in my pocket—I'd rather have had five dollars and someone to have a good time with. Then I got to thinking about whether you could have a good time with five dollars. It was boring on the stairs.

Whatever Harvey and Lulu did took about an hour and left Harvey looking as if he'd been dragged from the surf. He came lurching out with his shirt undone and his fly open. He smelled like an overused sauna.

'Never had annathin' like it,' he said. 'In-credible.'

'I got the impression you were regulars.'

'Huh? Oh, sort of. Coast clear? Less go, I need a drink.'

We went out into the lane and that's where they were waiting. Two big men which made four big men, except that one of the big men was drunk and he was my responsibility. One of them stepped forward, looked closely at Salmon and ignored me.

'Salmon, we're going for a trip.'

'He's not going anywhere,' I said.

'Shut up, you, You can go back inside and look at the tits, we don't want you.'

I guessed that the bloke who hadn't spoken was the real muscle so I moved a little closer to him which also took me back towards the door. I gave him a short, hard right well below the belt and brought my knee up as his crotch came down. He groaned and gripped himself there; the other one was reaching inside his coat for something but I had a gun in my waist holster at the back and it came out smoothly as I turned around. I jabbed it hard into the talker's neck and then pulled it back and held it a few centimetres from his nose.

'Get back against the wall, Salmon,' I said. 'What's the other one doing?' I was staring into my man's eyes trying to convince him that I'd pull the trigger if I had to. I seemed to succeed; he dropped his hand from his coat and stood very still.

'He's holding his balls,' Salmon said.

'You sober enough to kick them if he looks frisky?'

'Yeah,' he muttered. 'Where's those fuckin cops?'

'We could find some,' I said. 'What d'you reckon?'

'Now, what's the point?'

'Okay,' I moved the .38 a little closer to the nose. 'You see how things are. Mr Salmon's not vindictive. You and your mate can walk down there and turn the corner and go home or I can shoot you somewhere. What's it to be?'

'We'll walk,' he said.

I heard a shuffling step and then the dull sound of a hard kick being delivered and then another. A man groaned and whimpered. I held the gun steady.

'What?' I said.

'Nothin',' Salmon said. 'This one can crawl. Let's go.'

I moved back to the wall and we watched the guy who'd been kicked lift himself up off the ground and steady himself. Neither of them looked at us. They walked and hobbled down the lane and around the corner. Salmon and I went the other way out to the neon-lit street.

'You were good, Hardy.'

I grunted. 'Why'd you kick him?'

'I was feelin' good. He spoiled my night.'

The next day Salmon spent the morning in bed. He made a few phone calls in the afternoon, watched some TV. I went out and got some Chinese food and a paperback of *Dutch Shea Jnr* by John Gregory Dunne. We ate, I read; Salmon watched commercial television and went to bed early. I slept on the couch but not well; I spent most of the night reading and drinking instant coffee so that I'd finished the book by morning. Good book.

On Friday morning I told Salmon I needed some fresh clothes and wanted to go to the bank, so I had to get back to Glebe. That was all right with him because he wanted to go to Harold Park that night anyway. We had our discreet police escort over to Glebe, and I did my business with Salmon hanging around looking bored. Putting a couple of hundred in the bank to cover a mortgage payment probably wasn't a very big deal to him.

In the afternoon I watched some more of the tennis while Salmon yawned over some back-issue magazines he found in the living room.

'You miss these inside.' He flipped over the pages of a mid-year *National Times*.

'How did you find it? Prison, I mean.'

'Hot and hard. You ever been in, Hardy?'

'Not really, short remand at the Bay.'

He snorted derisively and seemed to be about to

say something. Then he yawned and turned another page. John Alexander was giving ten years away to Peter Doohan and the games were going with service.

About half an hour earlier than I'd have thought necessary, Salmon announced it was time to go.

'It's too early,' I said. 'It's just down the road.'

'I want to get a good park.'

'I thought we'd walk. Do you good.'

'No, We drive.'

He was paying. We drove. I like Harold Park; somehow, even though they put in new bars and generally ponced the place up a few years ago, they managed not to kill the atmosphere. With the lights and the insects swarming in the beams and the Gormenghast houses up above The Crescent, the track feels like a special place—just right for what happens there. The race call and announcements over the PA system boom and bounce around in the hollow so that everybody knows what's going on. You get a cheerful type of person at Harold Park—it's almost a pleasure to lose money there.

Some sort of change had come over Salmon. He was decisive about where he wanted us to park—out on The Crescent, well down from the Lew Hoad Reserve—and for the first time he showed a real interest in our police escort.

'Give 'em plenty of time to pick us up,' he said as I locked the car.

'If they're any good, they won't need help.'

'Just do as I say.'

We walked around to the main entrance in Wigram Road and I looked arcoss to the pub.

'That's it,' I said.

'What?'

'The Harold Park—the pub over there. Didn't you say it was one of the places you wanted to visit before you took your trip?'

Salmon glanced at the pub which was doing its usual brisk race-night business.

'Skip it,' he said nervously. 'The rozzers with us?'

They were, two guys in casual clothes looking like family men on a matey night out. They went through the turnstiles a few bodies behind us. I could feel the tension in Salmon as we stepped out of the light into an area of shadow in front of the stand.

'Okay,' he said. 'Now we lose 'em. Right now. We make for the exit over near the car.' He moved quickly, pushing through clutches of people heading for the bars and the tote; the mob swirled around us with no pattern yet, no fixed positions taken, and the gaps closed up behind us. I sneaked a look back after a while and caught a glimpse of the cops anxiously inspecting a toilet entrance.

Salmon moved fast on the way back to the car. He hugged the wall and people got out of his way.

'They're likely to leave someone watching the car?'

I considered it. We hadn't been evasive at any time, rather the reverse; anyone who knew my habits would wonder why I'd drive such a short distance, but not too many cops knew my habits.

'Doubt it, but there's no time for a recce. That pair'll be on our hammer pretty soon.'

'Right. Let's go.'

'Where?'

'North.'

I took Victoria Road to the Gladesville Bridge and ran up through the back of Pymble to pick up the turn-off to French's Forest. RBT seemed to have quietened Friday night down: the traffic moved smoothly and after Salmon got finished checking behind us for pursuit, he settled down and enjoyed the drive.

'Nice night.' he said.

'Yeah, where're we going?'

'Whale Beach.'

'Jesus, why?'

He gave a short laugh, one of the very few I'd heard from him. 'Not for a swim.'

The traffic stayed light on Barrenjoey, all the way past Newport to the Whale Beach turnoff. The Falcon handled the drive well, but Salmon only grunted when I commented on it.

'Fords are junk.' he said.

It was true that Fords weren't in abundance in the drives and on the road in front of the big houses. I saw Mercs and Jags, Celicas and the like, all looking good in the moonlight like the houses themselves. Salmon was concentrating on the terrain and when we reached a sign that said 'Public Pathway to Beach', he told me to stop.

'What's here?'

'Me cabin. Not too many know about it.'

We started down a steep and long flight of steps. I could see the water gleaming out ahead and heard the big surf crashing on the beach. About half of the houses were in darkness and the whole area was quiet and still apart from the sound of the sea and a few night birds calling. Halfway down the steps Salmon stepped over the rail and took a look into the blackness.

'Shoulda brought a torch,' he muttered.

'Don't you know the way?'

He glanced at me sharply. 'Sure, but it's been a while.'

We pushed through the bushes following a rabbit track until a squat shape loomed up in front of us. Salmon had taken his jacket off because the path ran slightly up and it was sweaty work on a mild night. He fumbled in a pocket and pulled out a bunch of keys. He handed me the jacket.

'Wait here, Hardy.'

I stood in the shadows holding the jacket and feeling like a five hundred dollar-flunky; then I remembered that it was a thousand dollar-flunky and felt better. Salmon went up some wooden steps and took a long time selecting a key and getting it into the lock. Then he opened the door and took a long time turning on a light. The jacket felt heavy because there was a .45 automatic in one of its pockets. It was a long time since my army days when we practised stripping guns in the dark but I found I could still do it. I kept an eye on the light in the cabin while I ejected the bullet from the chamber, turned the top bullet in the spring-loaded magazine around and effectively jammed the thing as tight as a seized piston.

When Salmon came out of the cabin he was carrying a small canvas bag and wearing a look of satisfaction. I handed him the jacket.

'Want me to carry the bag?'

'Sure.' He gave me the bag and we pushed our way back to the path. The bag felt full of something but light; maybe it was toilet tissue for his trip.

Back at the car, Salmon shrugged his jacket on and took the bag from me. I looked up at the starry sky out to sea.

'Nice place,' I said.

'Yeah.' He was waiting impatiently for me to open the car.

'Changed a bit in the last year or so though.'

'Yeah.'

We drove back to Erskineville in virtual silence; it was an easy drive which gave me plenty of time to think. As far as I knew, nothing had changed much in Whale Beach for years—the affluent and trendy locals wouldn't permit it.

Salmon stowed the bag away in the bedroom and we had a Scotch before going to our respective beds.

'What time's your flight?' I was contemplating another Scotch, mindful of the hardness of the sofa.

'Eleven in the morning.'

'All fixed up?'

'Yeah. Goodnight, Hardy, and thanks.'

I couldn't sleep. I lay awake thinking about it and trying to figure what was going on. I felt sure things weren't what they seemed but that didn't take me far. I dozed and jerked awake with the same doubts and confusions crowding my mind. I didn't care about Harvey Salmon one way or another; as far as I knew he hadn't ever killed anybody, and in the world of organised crime his speciality was more in the organisation than the criminality. Still, I didn't like being so much in the dark. Around 7 a.m. I called Harry Tickener, who writes on crime and politics for *The News*. He was grumpy about being woken up so early and I had to keep my voice low which made him even grumpier.

'What can you tell me about Harvey Salmon, Harry?'

'At 7 a.m. nothing.'

'Come on, I need something. I know what he looks like, six foot two, fourteen stone; what about habits and so on?'

'Shit, Cliff, I don't know. Wait'll I get a cigarette. Okay ... Well, fourteen stone's a bit heavy. I can't think of much, except that he's a tennis nut.

'What?'

'Tennis, played it all the time, had his own court and that.'

'Thanks, Harry.'

'Any other time, Cliff. Not 7 a.m.'

He rang off and I put the phone down carefully. I was trying to digest the information when my flatmate came through the door wearing striped pyjamas and pointing the .45 at me.

'Heard you on the extension,' he said. 'Careless.'

'You're not Harvey Salmon.'

'No, but I've got this and you're still going to do what I say.'

He didn't tell me his name but he told me about the deal over the next few hours as he packed his bags and we waited to go to Mascot. As he understood it, an elaborate arrangement had been arrived at between Salmon and the State and Federal police. Salmon wanted two things—a new identity and a new life in South America (that was one) and a chance to pick up a bag of money from Whale Beach. The Federal police wanted information; the State cops wanted convictions. Harvey Salmon was released on licence in return for certain information; he didn't trust the police and he knew about a lookalike who was doing time in Grafton jail for fraud. The deal was that the look-alike would move around Sydney for a few days under police protection so that the real Salmon could get an idea of how effective that might be.

'What about the bag of money?'

'Salmon was dead keen to get hold of that. The State cops okayed it; the Federals don't know about it.'

'Why would the cops make a deal like that? Salmon'd sung already.'

'Not the whole song.' Harvey Salmon said. 'He keeps the last few notes until he gets his tickets and the bag at the airport.'

'What d'you get?'

'Some money and my freedom.' He grinned. 'And Lulu. Christ!'

'You can go back for more.'

He shook his head. 'Deal is, I leave Sydney for good.'

'Tough.'

'Yeah, now give me that gun you flashed outside the club.'

I gave him the gun, he took the bullets out and put them in his pocket before returning it. That made two inoperative guns and quite a relaxed atmosphere as far as I was concerned.

'What do you know about the cops who were tailing us?' I said, just to pass the time.

He grinned again; he was getting more relaxed by the minute and if he kept on grinning he might turn from a sad spaniel to a happy kelpie. 'I'd guess they were State boys the other night.' he said. 'Didn't care too much if Salmon got roughed up. They would've been the Federals last night; they're not supposed to know about the money, but they couldn't follow Neville Wran down Macquarie Street, anyway.'

'Probably right. Whose idea was it to bring me in?'

'Mine. I heard about you from Clive Patrick.'

'Is he in Grafton?'

'Yeah, copping it sweet. Be out pretty soon.'

I nodded and thought it over. I could take over now; the .45 was a liability and I was sure I had more moves than whatever-his-name-was. But I thought I might as well see it through.

'What about the other five hundred dollars?' I said.

'At the airport—after the swap.'

I drove to the airport. He checked a suitcase through to Rio having collected his ticket and an envelope at the desk. He had a smaller bag as cabin luggage which was about the same size as the bag he'd collected at Whale Beach.

Pan Am flight 304 to Rio de Janeiro was on time and would be boarding in an hour. He got his seat allocated and was heading for the baggage security check when things started to happen. First, a tall man stepped in front of us and showed us his face. He had a long, droopy sort of face, baggy eyes and was built on leaner lines than my companion.

'I'm Salmon,' he said. 'Let's have the bag and the ticket.'

The false Harvey Salmon was looking nervous; he fumbled in his jacket for the ticket and seemed to be playing for time. Two men detached themselves from a knot of people looking at a flights monitor and strode over to us. They were big, wore expensive suits and had short haircuts. One of them gripped the real Salmon by the arm. 'Would you come with us, sir?'

Salmon gave the man a tired smile. 'It's okay. I've got it here.' He tapped his breast pocket.

'Just come along, sir, and you too, please.' He looked sternly at the impostor and me and fell in behind us like a sheep dog. I thought he'd be a pretty good heel snapper from the smooth confidence of his movements.

'Along here.' The man holding on to Salmon steered us across the floor and behind some shrubbery to a room marked 'Security'.

'What is this?' Salmon said. He got shoved firmly inside for an answer.

The room contained a desk with a chair drawn up to it and a row of chairs over by a big, bright window. The sun was shining in and throwing long shadows from the divisions in the window across the pale carpet.

'We're police,' the arm-holder said. 'If you and Mr Salmon would just go over there and sit down, please.' He struggled to frame the polite words and to keep his diction smooth. Under the barbering and suiting there was a very rough customer. Salmon looked alarmed and angry; he moved his hand towards his pocket again.

'I've got it here.'

'I'm sure you have.' the cop said. 'Sit down.'

We sat, not side by side but a few seats apart. Salmon had broken out in sweat. The second cop put the bag on the desk and opened it. He nodded and turned to the impostor.

'Good. Got your ticket?'

The look-alike nodded and the cop carefully extracted a bundle of notes from the bag and passed them to him. 'Harvey Salmon' counted them, separated some and walked over to me. He held out the money; I sat still and he dropped the notes in my lap.

'Thanks, Hardy. I've got a plane to catch.' He didn't look at Salmon; he turned and walked out of the room. Salmon stood up and rushed across to where the policeman was zipping up the bag.

'That's mine,' he yelped. 'We had a deal. I get the money and you get the names.'

The policeman shook his head slowly and his smile was as cold and cheerless as a Baptist chaplain. The second cop moved in behind Salmon to do some shepherding.

'You've got it wrong, Harvey,' the bag man said. 'We wanted the money and no one wanted the names. No one wants you either.'

The other cop nudged Salmon. 'Come on.'

'No!' Salmon spun around desperately and looked across the room at me. 'Help me!'

The cop swung the bag in his hand and smiled again. 'He's done all he can. Harvey Salmon's flown to Rio. Come on.'

Salmon sagged and one of them grabbed him and held on hard. I sat there with an empty gun in my pocket and five hundred dollars in my crotch and watched them leave the room.

Three days later I sat in the home of my friend, Detective Sergeant Frank Parker, and told him about it. The telling took a bottle of wine and set up a strong craving for one of Frank's cigarillos. I fought the craving; no sense losing all the battles. Frank listened and nodded several times while he smoked and poured the wine.

'It's pretty neat.' he said when I finished. 'Must've been a lot of money in that bag?'

'Where would that have come from d'you reckon?'

Frank leaned back and blew smoke up over my head. 'Let's see, I'd say it would have been grateful contributions from people Salmon had kept quiet about. Mind you,' he gave me the sort of smile you give when you read a politician's obituary, 'that's not to say that some of their names wouldn't have been on the final list he was going to hand over.'

'Jesus. I still don't feel good about watching him being carted away to be cancelled.'

'Nothing you could do. Describe the man in charge, Cliff.'

'Big,' I said. 'Six one or two; heavy but with a lot of muscle; smart suit; fresh everything—shave, haircut, the lot. Looked like he'd still be good at breaking heads and that he learned not to say "youse" and "seen" for "saw" not so long ago.'

Frank nodded and drew in smoke. 'He's an Armed Robbery "D". Henry "Targets" Skinner. His turn'll come.'

Tearaway

'He's a tearaway, Cathy,' I said. 'You know it, I know it, everybody knows it. The best thing you could do would be to forget him. Get out of Sydney; go to Queensland. Kevin's caused you enough misery for a lifetime, it's all he's good at.'

'He never hurt anybody,' she said stubbornly. 'Never. Not anyone!'

'Just luck. He carried a gun—he pointed it, he never fired it but that's just a matter of luck. One split second can change all that and make him a murderer. That's still on the cards.'

I thought I had to be hard on her, but it turned out I was too hard. She'd come to me for help; she tramped up the dirty stairs and down the gloomy corridor and knocked on my battered door and all I'd done was cause her to drop her head onto my desk and cry buckets. I never did have much tact—a private detective doesn't use it much—but this wouldn't do. I came around the desk and gave her a tissue and made her sit up and swab down. Her boyfriend, Kevin Kearney had broken out a police van two days before. Kev and his three mates were on their way to their trial for armed robbery. One of them was shot dead twenty feet from the van; Kevin and the other two had got away. He hadn't contacted Cathy which was probably the first good turn he'd done her.

When she'd stemmed the flow and got a cigarette going, Cathy filled me in on the shape and structure of her distress.

'He got word out to me that he was going to run. I got a car and some money and we were going . . .', she stopped and looked at me hesitantly.

'Call it Timbuktu, Cathy,' I said. 'What does it matter?'

'Well, I heard about the break on the news. Christ, I nearly died when they said one of them'd been shot. But . . .'

The cigarette wavered in her hand and she looked ready to cry again.

'It wasn't Kev,' I said gently. 'Go on.'

'That's all. He didn't come—no phone call, nothing.'

'I read about it. The cops say they've got no leads.'

She flicked ash; she was perking up a bit. 'Same here.' She opened her bag and took out a roll of notes and put them on the desk.

'Nine hundred bucks. It's the money we were going to shoot through on. Kev'd beat the shit out of me if he knew what I was doing, but I want you to find him.'

I looked at the money, thinking a lot but not saying anything. Cathy stubbed her cigarette out in an ashtray alongside the cash.

'Look, he's guilty, he'll get—what? Ten years? He'll serve—what? Six? That's not too bad. I can wait. On the run he's likely to get killed, and then I'd kill myself.' She grinned at me, finally showing some of the spark that made her one of the most popular whores in Glebe. 'You'd be saving two lives, Cliff.'

I grinned at her. 'When you put it like that, how can I refuse? But seriously, Cathy, it's bloody dangerous. Harbouring's a serious charge. One of them's dead, the cops won't really mind if they take out another couple.'

'I know. Just do what you can. He might've decided it was safer to go another way, he could be clear. I just want to know something.'

'All right.' I took the money; I didn't have any qualms about the way it had been earned—hell, I'd worked for doctors and lawyers; all manner of professional people.

'Where do you start?' Cathy said.

'With whoever it was gave you the nod about Kevin's break.'

That pulled her up short—it touched on the code of Cathy's world: don't name names, don't describe faces, don't take cheques. I waited while she lit up again.

'No way around it, love. It's the only way in.'

'Kevin wouldn't like it,' she blew smoke in a thin, nervous stream. 'Well, it was Dave Follan.'

She told where and when Follan drank, which was better than getting his address. I told her I'd stay in touch with her and report everything I learned straightaway. She came around the desk on her high heels, put her behind in its tight denim on the desk, leaned forward to give me the cleavage and kissed me on the cheek.

'That's like having fish fingers at Doyle's.'

'What?'

'Never mind. I'll do what I can, Cathy. But I tell you one thing, you contact me if Kevin gets in touch with you. I don't want him wandering around with the wrong ideas about me.'

'He's a sweet guy really.'

'Yeah.'

She left and I leaned back in my chair and thought about Cathy and Kevin. I'd known them both in Glebe since they were kids. Kevin wagged school, stole things and played reserve grade football where he learned to drink and fight. I saw him play for

Balmain a few times; I saw him in a police line-up and then I saw him in a car that belonged to someone else. I was working for the someone else at the time, so I had a talk to Kevin. His ideas about property were loose; he was apologetic but unfussed about the car. I took it away, and we parted with mutual respect.

Cathy's path to the game was the usual one—good looks, lazy parents, bored teachers, boring schools, no skills, good times. She was at it by fifteen, and nine years later the marks on her were plain. Cathy had seen and touched it all; raw life and death had pushed and shoved her. She'd pushed back with good humour and a generous heart and very little else. She once told me she'd never read a book, and had watched TV for seventy-two hours straight when she was stoned. Her pimp—who I didn't know was a pimp at the time—hired me to protect him from another pimp. It all got messy and I ended up protecting Cathy. Then she met Kevin and he took over all the work.

When you want information about crims, talk to the cops, and vice versa. They spend half their lives on the phone to each other. I called Frank Parker and asked him what he'd heard about the escapee Kevin Vincent Kearney.

'Not a thing.'

'His best girl's anxious.'

'So she should be. Is she willing to help us catch him before he does something silly?'

'Not exactly.'

'It was a sweet deal of a break, Cliff. In retrospect the van driver reckoned there could've been half a dozen cars on the roads blocking him and slowing him down. They had a nifty little jigger to cut the hole. That all takes money, and there's only one way to pay that sort of money back.'

'Yeah, I know.'

'Our ears're open, but there's nothing yet. What've you got?'

'Nothing.'

'Cliff, leave it alone. It's bound to be sticky. Do a few compo investigations, do a few arsons. Leave it alone.'

I grunted non-committedly and hung up.

In prison, men talk about escaping all the time. They talk about escapes that succeeded and those that didn't. They pool the knowledge, share the wisdom—the result is that they all do the same things when they're on the run and they mostly get caught. They talk endlessly about cars, which is one of the mistakes. Did you ever hear of anyone being apprehended in a taxi or a train? They steal cars and drive them in the dumb way they do everything else and they might as well be carrying a sandwich board—ESCAPEE AT LARGE.

Kevin was hooked on Volvos; he claimed they were safe, but no car was safe with Kevin at the wheel. Time was when a Volvo in Glebe would have stood out like a camel on Bondi beach, but that's all changed. Even so, it didn't hurt to cruise a few of Kevin's haunts—the gym off Derwent Street, the card room under the Greek restaurant in St John's Road, the Forest Lodge video outlet where Kev and the girls sometimes made their own movies—just in case there was a Volvo around that didn't belong. There wasn't, but it filled in the time until I could go looking for Dave Follan at the Glebe Grenadier.

The Grenadier is the sort of pub the Vicar warned you about—it smells of smoke and spilt beer and a good time. It used to serve counter lunches that would stop a wharfie but they cut them down when the weight-conscious professionals moved in. But there's a bus stop outside, a TAB next door, no stairs to the pisser—nothing will ever drive the old-timers from the Grenadier.

I ordered a beer and looked around for the pub's social secretary—the man or woman who would know everyone who came and went and the colour of their socks. He was leaning his belly against the bar and watching the pool players. People slapped him on the shoulder as they passed and he greeted them by name without even looking at them. He was the man. I eased up to him with money in my hand ready to order.

'Good pub,' I said.

'Usta be, too many bloody trendies now.'

The clientele looked pretty solidly working class to me, but I respected his judgement.

'Dave Follan's a regular here, isn't he? He's no trendy, Dave.'

'Need more of him.' He finished his schooner and I gave the barman the signal as soon as his glass hit the bar. I finished too and ordered a middy. He lit a cigarette in the small space between drinks.

'Ta.' he sipped. 'You a mate of Dave's?' He looked at me properly for the first time; his eyes were lost in the beer fat and his small mouth was overhung by a whispy ginger moustache. He wore no particular expression and it was impossible to guess at his thoughts.

'Sort of,' I said. 'Wouldn't happen to know if he's coming in tonight, would you?'

He reached over the bar and poured the rest of the schooner into the slops tray. When he turned back to me he was holding the empty glass like a weapon. 'I would happen to know. I'm Follan, and I don't know you from Adam, mate. What the fuck d'you want?'

After the Hardy foot, I thought, *try the Hardy*

charm. I grinned at him. 'Let me buy you a beer, I got off on the wrong foot then.'

He wasn't having any. 'You certainly did. What's your game?'

'Cathy told me you gave her the nod about Kevin's break.'

'Cathy should keep her bloody trap shut, then.'

'She's worried about Kevin, just wants to know he's okay.'

Follan's piggy eyes drifted along the bar to the right and left of us; it looked as if he could measure earshot to within an inch. He sucked froth from his empty glass and somehow I knew it was to oil a lie. 'I dunno any more than what I told Cathy. I got the word from a bloke who was just out. Kevin told him to look me up. I gave it to Cathy word for word and that's all I know.'

'I could be lying about Cathy, I could be a cop.'

He signalled for more beer. 'Who gives a shit? I dunno where Kevin is.'

'That's a good safe story you've got.'

'It's true, too. Piss off.'

I downed my drink and walked away; before I left the bar I turned and looked back. Follan was jiggling his change like a man about to make a phone call. I walked up the street and moved my car to a point where I could see the pub door, but was hidden behind three or four cars. I was hungry and the two quick middies felt like a gallon on my empty stomach. A taxi pulled up immediately outside the bar door and Follan took three steps across the pavement and got in. 'If you drink, don't drive'—an honest citizen observing the law? Not likely; I U-turned dangerously and followed the taxi.

After fifteen years in the business of doing for people what they can't do for themselves, I thought nothing a human being did could surprise me. Follan proved me wrong; I thought he'd head for some Ultimo or Chippendale boarding house, or another pub, but the taxi drove to the Bellevue Hotel. Follan got out and waddled into the foyer as if he belonged there. I couldn't park and I didn't fancy hanging around behind aspidistras in the lobby anyway. I drove home, had a sandwich and some wine and sat out behind the house looking at the big city glow and smelling the big city smells. They jangle some people; they soothe me.

Dave Follan looked at me sullenly. I'd followed him from the Grenadier the next day to his flat in Avon Street, Glebe. I'd bailed him up as soon as he turned the key, pushed him in, and tried to impress him with my seriousness as much as with the .38. But I wasn't sure it was working. He sat on an overstuffed, floral covered chair and looked belligerent. The flat was fussily decorated and arranged but the arrangements were fraying and breaking down as if the woman who'd set them up was no longer around. Fat Dave Follan looked incongruous amid the floral prints and china, but he didn't seem to know it.

'You won't use that bloody thing,' he growled. 'I'm just sittin' here wondering where to hit you.'

'It could come to that,' I said evenly. 'After we spoke the other day you made a phone call and then you went to the Bellevue. I want to know why.'

'You know what you can do.'

I took off my jacket and put the gun in the pocket, dropped the jacket over a chair. 'You're fat and I've got ten years on you. You'll get hurt and we'll break things. You really want to do it this way?'

'Yes.' He came up out of the chair heavily but not too slow. He expected his bulk to help but it didn't. He swung at me, I moved aside and he nearly lost balance.

'You've had a few too many as well, Dave. Don't push it.'

He swore and drove a pretty good punch straight at me. I took it on the shoulder moving back. He was slow to recover and I put my bunched right hand in his face, fingers near the eyes and the heel on the nose and pushed hard. He grunted and went down.

'This is silly,' I said. 'But if that's the way you want it, okay. I'll fix you up here, go to the Bellevue, find out what room you went to, give it a call and throw your name in. Be interesting to see what pops up.'

That got to him. The beer courage and the bully drained out of him. He got up slowly and eased onto the couch; his flesh spread and settled as he let it take his weight. That left him with the weight on his mind.

'Don't do that. Jesus, don't do that.'

I picked my jacket off the chair and sat down. 'Well, you can see where we are, Dave. You have to tell me why you're so scared.'

'I'm a dead man if I bloody do,' he muttered.

'It's up to you, maybe I can keep you out of it. I could try. D'you have any choice?'

He shook his head. 'Wish the missus was here; I could do with a cuppa.'

'Where is she?'

'Dead. Month back.'

'Get on with it, Dave.'

His cigarettes had fallen on the floor and he reached down for them; the effort brought the blood back to his face, and I watched him scramble and wheeze until he had one lit. 'Big job on, of course. Interstate money.'

'Where from?'

'North. Kevin and the others are gonna do it. Cost

money to get 'em out.'

'Why them?'

'It's a fuckin' cowboy job, that's why. You'd have to be bloody desperate to try it. They'll have other guns on 'em while they re doin' it. I picked that up by accident, wasn't supposed to.'

'Where and what?'

He sucked on his cigarette and let the smoke out slowly. 'I don't know, that's the truth.'

He could have been lying, it was impossible to say; he was going to lie at some point, I was sure of that.

'Why the message to Cathy?'

'That was a blind; Kevin reckoned she'd get a car and get some dough together. The cops'd watch her and he could stay outa sight—keep clear of her.'

'Where?'

'Don't know.'

That was all I'd get from him, I knew. We were manoeuvring each other; he'd said enough to make it not worthwhile for me to blow him to his principals; but if the worst happened and he had to front them he could claim he hadn't sung the whole song. They might leave him a toe.

I pulled on my jacket and shoved the gun in under my arm. 'I've got you by the balls, Dave. I can drop you in it with the cops or the other side. You know that?'

He nodded. 'Why would you?'

'I wouldn't need a reason. Last thing—give me the number at the Bellevue. That's it, just three little words.'

'Five oh six.'

'I thank you. You're on your own now, Dave. You'd better play it by ear.'

If you've got the room number, fifty dollars will get

you the name of any hotel resident in the city. Room 506 at the Bellevue was occupied by a Mr Carpenter of Southport. My informant, who arranged transport for the guests and did a stint on the desk, threw in for free a physical description and that Mr Carpenter would be leaving the hotel at 10 a.m. the following day. He was new at the job—he could have negotiated that into another twenty.

The example of Dave Follan turned me off drinking for the night. I went to a film that tried to make me cry; it didn't, but it could have. I walked up through Hyde Park to Darlinghurst to drink coffee worth walking that far for. The blocking of the streets has caused the girls to move to William Street where they seemed to be crowding each other a little. In Darlinghurst you do it in a terrace bedroom rather than the back seat of a car, but it's the same thing. I thought about Cathy who made calls and went out to dinner more these days, but that's the same too.

Ten o'clock found me illegally parked and alert outside the Bellevue Hotel. Carpenter was easy to spot—a beefy, florid guy wearing a beige safari suit that might have cost five hundred bucks but still looked like a rag. He put two sizable suitcases into a new Falcon wagon and we were off. My ancient Falcon followed the new model like a discarded bull trying to keep up with the new leader of the herd.

The drive wasn't far and wasn't scenic. The Falcon pulled up outside a blighted-looking terrace house in Enmore on the Newtown side. It was as unneighbourly a house as you'll see around there—on a corner, with an empty factory next door and the railway across the street. The house was a grimy, crumbling hulk, but it had one big advantage—you could get away from it in at least four different directions, and one route, by the tunnel under the railway, would take care of a pursuing car.

One of the plusses for my car is that it can look abandoned. I sat in it, hunched down, about four houses and two rusty galvanised iron fences away and watched the house. Two kids who should have been at school wandered past and looked incuriously at me. A dog helped things along by pissing casually against the front wheel, rubbing himself briefly on the tyre and ambling off. After a while a car pulled up outside the house, two men alighted and went inside. Pretty soon they all came out: Carpenter, the two new arrivals and three other men, one of whom was Kevin Kearney.

Kevin had grown a beard, lost weight and dyed his hair three shades darker, but his cocky walk, compensating for the fact that he was only five foot six, and the aggressive set of his shoulders was unmistakable. The party split up between the wagon and the car with Kevin riding separately from Carpenter. I had a moment's worry, but it passed—the cars followed the same route.

We drove in convoy to Five Dock. They pulled up within sight of the Great Western Highway intersection at a place where the canal goes under the road and there is a wide dividing strip and big grassy stretches on either side of the road. Houses are few and back where the priorities of highway and park have pushed them. I drove on and took a turn after the canal so that I could come back on the other side of the water and watch the group safely from pretty close quarters. The two parties coalesced, then split again. Carpenter and Kearney went towards the highway; Carpenter looked to be talking fast. The others broke into two pairs and moved around on opposite sides of the road. The two men who'd arrived later in Enmore went up a grassy bank to a high point above the road. A concrete bridge crossed another loop of the canal up there and they stood by it, looking down at the road and Kevin's two mates who smoked, glanced up and down the road and looked anxious.

Carpenter and Kearney joined them and Kevin did some nodding. Where they stood was a collection of yellow and black striped council gear—uprights, reflector lamps, long wooden bars—just the stuff for traffic diversion and road blocking. Carpenter turned and looked at the two by the bridge and Kevin's eyes followed his.

The two hill climbers came back down, the smokers stamped out their butts and everyone climbed aboard again for the ride back to Enmore. Carpenter's car peeled off and headed towards the city but Kevin and his mates were delivered safely home just as the westbound 12.45 rattled past their front door.

I was pushing my luck by trailing the other pair once they'd deposited the fugitives, but I risked it. They drove to Annandale and disappeared into a trucking yard. The sign on the fence said that interstate and international freight was handled there. The curious thing was that I had a sense of having picked up a tail myself on this run. I tested the feeling around an Annandale block or two, but I was either wrong or it dropped off. It was something else to think about on the way back to Glebe for a late lunch and a very late drink.

Some of it wasn't hard to understand. The job was a hi-jack with no honour among thieves. Kevin and the boys were going to be under surveillance; Carpenter was putting up the money. Three things were unknown: what the cargo was, why Follan had called it a 'cowboy' operation and why Kevin hadn't been in touch with Cathy. She wasn't green; she would probably have driven the prime mover for Kevin if he'd asked her. The biggest question of all was—what was I going to do about it?

The first move was to get in touch with Kevin, and I didn't fancy doing that by driving up to the door. I sent him a telegram—to the name Kevin Vincent at the address in Enmore. I asked him to phone me and to keep everything under his hat; Kevin'd like that—there was an old-fashioned streak in him. His call came at a bit after five.

'Haven't seen you for a bit, Cliff. Have you still got all your hair, boy?'

'Yes, Kevin. And your phoney brogue's as bad as ever. But I'll play along—why do you ask?'

'Because you've got a lot to keep under your own bloody hat and I wondered if there'd be the room, like?'

'Knock it off, Kevin. You're about to do something very silly.'

'What would you know about it?'

I thought about telling him but decided against it; Kevin was inclined to be irrational when he was angry. 'It stands to reason. You've got a job lined up.'

'How'd you get on to me?'

'A whisper. Cathy asked me to look for you. She's worried and she's got good cause. She says she'll wait for you to serve the five or six.'

The laugh that came across the line wasn't the old feckless Kevin laugh. It was harsh and bitter, and had not a shred of amusement in it. A prison laugh, maybe.

'Wait? Cathy? Her idea of waitin's to only be taking on one at a time.'

I didn't say anything; I was more interested in listening.

'Well, Cliff,' he said. 'You can tell her I'm in the

pink ... shut up!' I heard a short laugh and a scuffling sound, then Kevin went on in a steady voice. 'And I'll be in touch soon. She's not to worry.'

'Oh yeah, great! She'll eat that up, Kevin. That'll fix everything.'

'Soon means soon.'

'How soon?'

'Tomorrow.'

Jesus, I thought, *it's tonight*.

'Now, Cliff, you just get yourself a bottle of something good and settle down for a quiet night with your books. You hear me, Cliff? Get nosey and you're history. Got it?'

'Yeah.' He rang off, and I sat there holding the phone and thinking it had been one of the least productive conversations of my life. The three unknowns were still unknown and I still didn't know what I was going to do. I phoned Cathy, couldn't get her and chased her unsuccessfully through four telephone numbers, leaving urgent messages for her to call me.

The temptation to do as Kevin suggested, hit the bottle, was immense but I fought it. I had one big Scotch and left it at that. I spoiled some eggs trying to make an omelette of them, ate the mess and felt bad. Towards the back of my brain a voice was telling me to call Frank Parker, but I kept getting a picture of Kevin with his beard and dyed hair and I couldn't do it.

When the call came I nearly hurdled a chair to snatch up the phone. It was Cathy; she told me to wait until she came over, which would be in about an hour. She sounded steady and she didn't want to hear anything I had to say.

It was after ten when she arrived—in a black velvet jacket and white silk pants. Her face was unnaturally pale and her eyes were over-dilated and bright. She had a bottle of Black Label Scotch with her and she invited me to pour her a big one before she draped herself on the couch in my living room. She lit a cigarette and stubbed it out straightaway, as if she didn't want to obliterate the odour of sex that clung to her. She drank some Scotch and arched up her shoulders and wriggled.

'I've been screwing my brains out,' she said.

'Is that right? It made you hard to find—I spoke to Kevin today.'

She drank some more, then she put the glass down and assumed a mock demure pose; she half-closed and dimmed her eyes and pressed her knees together. It disconcerted me; I wondered if she was drunk, but her co-ordination seemed perfect and she appeared to be under tight control.

'Tell me everything about it.'

'Well, he's in Sydney ... and, ah ... he hasn't been in touch for a good reason. He thought the cops'd be watching you and ...'

'I'm a sort of decoy, is that right?' She said it brightly but with an edge of hate.

'I knew you wouldn't like it.'

'It's not so bad.' She picked up her drink and took a hefty belt. 'I always liked you, Cliff. Why don't I just slip into your shower and then nip into your bed? You know, I can make it seem like I never did it before.' She laughed. 'Or only once or twice. What d'you say?'

Any other time I'd have been tempted. I can be a sucker for fantasy and I hadn't been to bed with a woman that month or the month before. But the ulterior motive was just a bit too obvious.

'Cut it out, Cathy. This is a serious situation.'

Her mood changed instantly. She knocked off the rest of the Scotch and stood up abruptly. 'I'm going to have a shower anyway, to wash off the last of you bastards.'

Water ran; she had an instinct for where bathrooms were. I put some more Black Label in my glass and waited for her to come back clean and explain to me. I seemed to do a fair bit of that—waiting to be explained to—and it sometimes made me feel like a foreigner with an imperfect grasp of the language.

The make up was gone when she came back; her hair was damp and she'd pulled the exotic clothes on as if they were a sweater and jeans. She looked, without the gloss, tough in a different way. She made herself another drink and got a cigarette going.

'I know all about it,' she said.

I stared at her.

'I mean, I know about the job. Five Dock?'

I nodded. 'How?'

She drank and her smile reminded me of Kevin's laugh over the phone—no fun in it. 'I knew you were good, that you'd find something, but I wasn't sure you'd be straight with me. So I had someone not as good as you trailing you around. He reported in to me this afternoon—all the details. It wasn't hard to work out what the job was. D'you know what they're lifting?'

I shook my head.

She gave that smile again and held up both hands. 'This, and this—booze and smokes. It's a hot load, going to get hotter. So you don't have to worry about honest citizens getting hurt.'

'How do you know all this?'

'Wasn't hard once I knew it was trucks and who the Queensland money was.' She looked at her watch. 'It's a pretty dumb game though—bloody well-guarded that shipment'll be. You did some good snooping, Cliff. The other bloke was impressed —you didn't spot him?'

'Maybe. Just at the end. Couldn't be sure. Cathy . . . did you try to talk Kevin out of this?'

She shook her head and drew on her cigarette.

'Why not? I did.'

'What did he say?'

'Not interested. Seemed very sure of himself.'

She consulted her watch again.

'Why d'you keep doing that?'

She got up. 'You won't go to bed, least you can do is take a girl for a drive.'

We were rolling past the Leichhardt Town Hall when she told me. 'You won't be able to get too close,' she said. 'It'll all be staked out. I told the cops.'

'God, Cathy! Why?'

She didn't answer; she just sucked on her cigarette and stared ahead through my dirty windscreen.

It was near midnight and a mist was rising off the canals and grass. Wednesday night, quiet, a good night for crime. The question of getting close never arose because it all happened as we skirted the park. The highway turn-off was in full view and I saw the high shape of a semi-trailer heading down the road. Then lights pointed crazily to the sky and there were flashes and flares out of the darkness. There was a sputtering of bright orange from up the hill where I'd seen the two heavies reconnoitring. The truck seemed to meander slowly down the grade, then pick up speed abruptly. Too abruptly: it skidded, lurched and rolled. There were dark shapes moving fast from the park and pairs of headlights suddenly cut through the dark mists. I stopped and braked without knowing it; the whole thing seemed to take an age with each separate part occupying its own bit of time, but in fact it must have been all over within a couple of minutes.

Cathy sat still and stared, and then she jumped and swore as her cigarette burned down to her fingers. She jerked open the door.

'What're you doing?' I reached across for the handle.

'I want to see. I was the fizzgig, I've got the right!'

'Don't be a fool! You don't know what's going to happen. Who's dead, who's alive. You know what'll happen to you if they find out you put them in.'

She broke my grip on the handle and opened the door. 'Who cares?' she said.

I got out and followed her down the road and across a broad strip of grass. We were challenged a hundred yards from the scene by a shape that rose up from behind a bush. Cathy walked unblinkingly towards the gun.

'I want to see Matthiesson,' she said.

The cop fell in behind us and we went the rest of the way to the overturned truck and the cars each with flashing warning lights and one blue eye blinking tracers of light over still and moving figures.

Matthiesson was a bulky man in a flak jacket and bullet proof gear. He held an automatic rifle and let its muzzle point to the ground when he saw Cathy.

'You shouldn't be here,' he said. 'And who's this?'

'A friend,' Cathy said dully. 'Where's Kevin?'

'He was hit. I'm sorry. I told you I couldn't make any promises.'

'Yes, you did. I want to see him.'

Matthiesson guided us across behind the truck. One of its wheels was still turning slowly and bits of gravel were still falling from it. The overturned truck smelt strongly of liquor, and there were rivulets running from it and soaking into the small, dark, twisted shape on the ground. Kevin was on his back; his face was blotched with blood and one eye socket was a brimming pool. He looked like the death photo of Bugsy Spiegel. Cathy looked down at him and the tears started and fell down her face and onto the body. She just stood there, slightly bent over, and looked and wept. I moved over, put my arm around her and gently eased her away; she went, on feet that moved in a slow, hobbled shuffle.

Sirens started howling and the ambulances arrived and a team came to right the truck. There was a lot of swearing and one scream of pain as someone with bullets in him was moved. I got Cathy back to my car, gave her a cigarette and drove back to Glebe. She resisted nothing, accepted everything. Her shoes had blood on them and I made her kick them off at the door. I sat her down and wiped her face and made us both a drink. She drank it in a gulp and held out the glass for more.

'You asked why?'

I nodded.

'I went there to see him this afternoon. To Enmore. Just as I got there this girl came out. Great tall thing, all in pink. Kevin always liked them tall, pink's his favourite colour. Kevin came out with her. His hair was different and he had a beard. He shaved it off, did y'see?'

I nodded again.

'He came out with her and I watched.'

'Cathy, you couldn't be sure. She might have been with one of the other blokes. Anything . . .'

'She copped his special big feel just before she got into her car. I should know. I know what it meant.'

I didn't say anything.

'That's it,' she said. 'That's why.'

What Would You Do?

I missed a forehand volley that came at me slow, loopy and as big as a basketball. That gave Terry the set 6-2 which was at least two games more than she usually beat me by. But then, she's a professional and I'm a roughie; she says she only plays me to get practice against a kicking serve and a good lob.

'No lobs,' she said as we walked off the court. 'You were lousy. What's wrong, Cliff?'

'I've got a problem.'

'Tell me about it.'

'Later.'

Later turned out to be quite a lot later. We were in my bed, slick with massage oil and sweat. Terry had come and I hadn't but that was all right. Sometimes it was the other way around, sometimes both of us came, sometimes neither. It was all good. Terry put a pillow on my shoulder and nestled her head in there; she put her hand between my legs.

'We've got all night,' she said. 'Let's hear it.'

Finding young missing persons is either easy or impossible. Many of them want to be found, and all you have to do is locate a friend and squeeze a little. Other names and addresses pop out like pips and the kid turns out to be living on junk food three blocks from home. The hard ones stay hard: the boy or girl goes a long way off and goes for ever. Mothers weep.

The Portia Stevenson case looked like a hard one.

Jessie Stevenson of Cammeray was a woman in her late thirties who worked hard at looking ten years younger and did pretty well at it. She came into my office wearing a tailored white suit, high heels and a lot of subtle make up. She slipped into the clients' chair and put her nice legs nicely on display.

'I hope it's not painful to you to mention this,' she said, 'but your ex-wife recommended you to me when she heard about our problem. We go sailing together, you see.'

'It's not painful. How is Cyn?'

'Oh, she's wonderful. She's married to Simon Theodore, he's . . .'

'In advertising. Yes, I know. If she's sailing she must have got over her sea sickness. That's wonderful—I'm glad. Tell me about the problem, Mrs Stevenson.'

'Jessie, please. After all Cynthia's told me, I feel I know you.'

I thought Cyn's version of our marriage would be a tale of bottles and battles, signifying nothing, but perhaps I was wrong.

'Jessie,' I said.

'I've got a seventeen-year-old daughter. Her name is Portia. I haven't seen her for three months. She hasn't been at school and none of her friends know where she is. There's been nothing—not a card or a phone call. Nothing. The police have done all the things they do. Nothing.'

'Any trouble with her? I mean before she went?'

'Oh, the usual—sulks, squabbles about money and going out. Nothing to speak of. She was a normal teenager. I've exhausted myself thinking about what might have made her go. I can't come up with anything. I've been distraught. I'm on medication now.'

There seemed to be an unnatural air to her—a

combination of a surface over-alertness and a background dullness. She spoke flatly, without emotion, as if that part of her response had been blocked off or re-routed. I judged her to be very vain and very troubled—not a good combination.

'I'll need quite a few things, Jessie. An introduction to someone at her school, a picture of course, a handwriting specimen, and I'll have to have a pretty thorough session with you and her father to go over her life. Runaway kids usually run back to something—some memory, something like that.'

'Her father's dead. He was killed in an accident when Portia was little. I re-married a few years later—Jeff's been like a father to her for ... nearly ten years.'

'Okay. When can I come out to see you both? Oh, any other kids?'

She shook her head. 'I'm going sailing this afternoon. I *think* Jeff's home tonight. You could come tonight.'

She gave me the address in Cammeray and we fixed on 8.30 for my visit. She got up and moved to the door; she was tall and she moved well but with that same distracted style, as if not all of her was really there. She transferred the leather drawstring bag she carried to her right hand in order to use the left to open the door. *Left-handed*, I thought, big advantage for tennis. I wondered if the kid was left-handed too; I was already working on the case—but not quite yet.

'Can I get a cheque from you tonight?' I asked.

She hesitated and her composed mask dropped momentarily; behind it there was confusion and distress to spare.

'Oh, I'm sorry, Mr Hardy. Yes, yes, of course. Jeff will give you a cheque. Whatever you ask, anything ...'

'Cliff,' I said. 'There's a standard rate. I'll see you tonight.'

She went out and I made a few notes and then picked up the phone. Good manners and good sense required me to contact the missing persons department in the police force. I've never encountered a competitive feeling from the cops in these matters; they have too many cases on their files to care about a private enquiry into one of them. Their manpower is stretched thin and a case they can cross off the books is just so many more hours they can put in elsewhere. The case officer on the Stevenson matter was Detective Constable Burns, and she was as nice as pie.

'Not a whisper,' she told me. 'The girl was doing quite well at school.' She named a north shore private school better known for placing its students in the society pages than the professions. 'Reasonable student, they said. We tracked down five or six friends, nothing. Just didn't turn up at school one day.'

'Boyfriends?'

'Not really. She went out a couple of times with a kid from Shore. Bit of a wimp. Didn't know a thing. Wouldn't have been one of the bunch with an income under a hundred thousand.'

I grunted. 'You checked the usual?'

'All negative: horses, drugs, booze, religion—all negative.'

'What did she take?'

'Clothes, records, video cassettes.'

'Diary?'

There was a silence at the other end, then she spoke slowly. 'No mention of any diary, no.'

'What did you make of the parents?'

'Rock solid. The stepfather's a partner in an ad agency, doing well. The mother...'

'Fills in her time.'

'That's right. Sailing, aerobic dancing, bit of gardening, reads a lot. Looks after herself.'

'Thanks. Did she have a bank account, Portia I mean. Christ, what a name!'

Detective Constable Burns laughed. 'Yeah, she hated the name. Called herself Ann. She had a passbook savings account with a couple of hundred bucks in it—didn't even take the book. It's a tough one, and you know the toughest part?'

'Tell me.'

'She made it in one jump. Usually they have a dry run or two and you can get a line on what's bugging them and what they're likely to do. Not Portia. She wouldn't have spent ten nights away from home in the last ten years, the way they tell it.'

'Over-protected?'

'Could be.'

I thanked her and put the phone down. What she'd told me jelled pretty well with what I knew from the missing persons cases I'd handled over the past fourteen years. Not many of them had been juveniles, but the principles were the same. A high proportion of the runaways just wanted to get attention—the run was a call for help; some had reached a temporary impasse in their lives and used the run to break the log-jam and get some movement going from which they could draw comfort or a course of action. A few go for good; they go a long way off, burrow and pull the hole in over them. A few meet with foul play and it worried me that no one had made any mention of that so far.

I read over a selection of cases including the handful of juveniles, made some notes and put through some calls to get a picture of the Stevensons. Jeff Stevenson was a partner in Armstrong & Stevenson, which was a biggish advertising agency with an office in North Sydney. His credit rating was tops, and his firm had good accounts with brewers and distillers and other pillars of our social life like a Japanese car manufacturer and a Taiwan-based toy importer.

It was mid-winter, which meant that Sydney turned on fine, bright days, ideal for tennis-playing in the morning and afternoon, but cold and dark by 5 p.m. In the mid-afternoon I drove out to Castlecrag to take a look at the school. The suburb's roads have military names like The Ramparts and The Bastion and the area has a defensive, fortressed look. The wealth and property behind the high walls and beyond the deep, verdant gardens would be worth defending.

The school looked like a stately home, somewhat on the large side. It boasted a high wall and massive gate house; the main building was a rambling, pseudo-Georgian affair with enough ivy on it to camouflage Ayers Rock. Playing fields stretched away and flagstoned paths wound between tennis courts, garden beds and an artificial pond.

I took this in from my car which I stopped on the other side of the road from the huge iron gates, and from a stroll along the west perimeter. As I watched, the place came to life. Schoolgirls suddenly spilled out of the main building from a couple of doors and started straggling along the paths—some towards the main gate and others off to two new buildings in the far distance which I took to be dormitories. I wondered if things had changed in the dorm since *Anne Of Green Gables*, a book of my sister's which I'd read with guilt and longing.

Even a brief loiter outside a girls' school is difficult to explain, so I moved the car a hundred yards to where I could observe a few of the novitiate socialites heading for the bus stop. They ranged in age from about twelve to seventeen; they wore a uniform—dark-blue tunic with white trimming and a hat—but most had managed to contrive some individuality through the cut of the clothes and the accessories. Some were trying for a Boy George look, others opted for Princess Diana. They fell over each other, screamed, punched and lounged at the bus stop as if their parents weren't paying two thousand bucks a term.

I drove a half-circuit of the school grounds and spotted the stables which had been mentioned in a booklet called *Selecting Schools in NSW* which I'd picked up in a newsagent. The establishment boasted a gymnasium, swimming pool, computer room, archery range, putting green, film and video studios and a theatrette. Social contacts with the leaders of tomorrow at the brother school were encouraged: unless she was on heroin or heavily into S&M, it didn't sound like such a bad place for a seventeen-year-old girl to be.

The light was failing; I needed petrol, a drink, some food and coffee and time to prepare myself to meet the Stevensons on their home ground. It was partly a matter of steeling myself for the flock of photographs, tattered toys and possible tears, and partly of repressing prejudice—rich ad men of Cammeray are not birds of my feather.

I drove to a pub in Mosman which I remembered for its roast beef sandwiches, house claret and quiet clientele. I was dressed for the weather and the company in woollen shirt, leather jacket, cords and not-so-old Italian shoes. Very Mosman. The pub had changed; it was crowded with under-age drinkers forking out for double bourbons and coke and puffing their way through packets of 30s. The sandwiches had given way to a junk food bar, and a glass of wine cost a dollar fifty. I had one with a packet of chips and let the music batter me senseless. I wondered if any of the girls spent their days behind the high walls and what went on under the wigs and dyed hair. A young woman done up like a gypsy in a variety of colours and fabrics with a fringed skirt that brushed the floor in places, bumped me and spilled her drink.

'Ooh, sorry,' she said.

'Your drink, not mine. Let me get you another one.'

Her black-rimmed eyes opened wide. 'Why?'

'Ask you a question in return. What're you having?'

'Brandy'n coke. Ta.'

She stood with her back to a wall and waited while I got the drink. I handed it to her and took a good look at her olive-skinned face: it was unlined and fresh despite the goo around her eyes and on her mouth. She had strong, white teeth and three studs in the lobe of each ear. She thanked me again and took a sip.

'What's the question, then?'

'What matters most in the world to you?'

She laughed. 'Thought you were gonna ask m'age. Let's see, now.' She lookd around the jam-packed room where bodies moved fractionally and the noise was like an endless, deafening echo. 'That's pretty easy, really. The most important thing in the world to me is to have a bloody, bloody, bloody good time. Bye.'

'Good luck.'

The Stevensons' house backed onto the water of Long Bay and was designed to take advantage of that fact. It seemed to have very little purchase on the land at all, but to be straining off the cliff face towards the water. It was the last house in row of similarly poised structures. I parked where the narrow, winding street wound least, and walked back towards the house. Even at the front gate I could hear water slapping at boats and the creaking of ropes. A short path took me through a determinedly native garden to the wide verandah that ran along the front of the house. I knocked at the door at 8.30 precisely and Jessie Stevenson answered it as if she'd been standing inside with her hand on the knob.

'Cliff, thank you for coming.'

I nodded and followed her down a passage to a sun room where the back of the house swooped out over the water. A tall, heavily built man lumbered up off a cane lounge as Jessie waved me through.

'Jeff, this is Cliff Hardy.'

He was wearing two pieces of a three-piece suit and had loosened his tie. His thinning dark hair was expensively barbered and his shoes were highly polished. The cut of the pants and waistcoat kept him from looking portly, which he was. His grip was stronger than it needed to be and his palm was moist.

'Hi. Drink?'

'Thanks,' I said. 'Red wine?'

'Coming up.' He went to the corner of the room where there was a bar in vaguely Hawaiian mood—bamboo and wickerwork with two high, spindly-legged stools. Jessie sat down on the lounge and picked up a pink drink from the low table in front of it. Stevenson came back with a glass of red and a can of beer which he popped as he sat down next to his wife. He had a long swig and she took hold of his free hand. As I sat opposite them in the quiet house with my drink in my hand, I saw two things: he was younger than her by a good few years and that was one of her problems; the other problem she was confidently expecting me to solve.

On the table was a folder that had my name written on it; it would be the memorabilia for sure. I took out a notebook and pen and placed them by the folder. I took a sip of the good red.

'First, does either one of you have any theory, doesn't matter how way out, about why she left?'

They looked at each other and shook their heads. 'She's a normal, healthy, lovely girl,' Stevenson said.' 'We never had any trouble with her.'

Jessie nodded and drank some of the pink mixture. 'I've thought about it for hours. Nothing comes, nothing.'

I touched the folder. 'The photographs and such?'

They nodded in unison and I opened the folder. 'The photographs ranged over about ten years, chronicling Portia from a gap-toothed kid to a tall, well-proportioned teenager. She had her mother's features and figure which were good credentials. Her hair shone in the outdoors pictures and there was a sultriness to her when photographed indoors that suggested she knew what it was to be a focus of attention. I murmured 'Very pretty' which was probably less than was expected of me, and went on with the other documents. There were a couple of school reports—just this side of glowing; Portia is steady and reliable etc., and a postcard she'd sent from Brisbane. Jessie Stevenson watched me while I read the dutiful message.

'She stayed with my sister,' she said. 'Just for a week.'

I nodded. There was a typed list of names, six females and two males.

'They're her closest friends,' Jeff Stevenson said. 'The police talked to them all.' His wife let go of his hand and stroked his arm. He turned his face to her and gave her a stiff smile. She kept her hand on his arm. The telephone number of the school and the names of some teachers were typed on another sheet. There was a photostat copy of the missing persons report the Stevensons had given to the police. It was an official form, listing ages and occupations, and told me nothing new. I returned the things to the folder and closed it.

'Did Portia keep a diary?' I asked.

The look they exchanged was uncertain; maybe they were swingers who feared that their daughter had chronicled the frolicking, but the way Jessie hung on to her husband's arm suggested she was anything but a swinger.

'No,' she said. 'Why do you ask?'

'Oh, I don't know. I just thought with the name—Portia, and everything—and with Jeff being an ad man, there might be a literary leaning in the family. Diaries are useful . . .'

'Portia was my mother's name,' Jessie said frigidly. Jeff was looking hostile, maybe he thought I'd maligned his profession by suggesting that it had anything to do with literature. I still liked the thought, though.

'Are her school books here?'

Jessie nodded.

'May I see them?'

'The policewoman had a good look,' Stevenson growled.

'Even so, I'd like a look if I may. And I'd like to see her room, please.'

Stevenson gently shook off his wife's hand. 'That's okay, of course, you'd want to do that. Drink up, Hardy. Jess'll show you the room. If you'll excuse me, I've got a couple of calls to make.'

He got up slowly and drained his can. He wasn't much over thirty but something was taking a toll of him—self-indulgence or business worries. There were strain lines in his fleshy face and his colour was too high. He moved rather slowly, like an ex-athlete who has stiffened up. I drank some more of the wine, put the glass on the floor, and followed Jessie back down the passageway.

She pushed open the second door along and flicked the light on. The bedroom was scrupulously tidy, the way no seventeen-year-old could have kept it. The bed was made, the rug was straight, the books were lined up, the cassettes were stacked. The room was already beginning to feel like a mausoleum. I opened a wardrobe and looked at the solid bank of clothes, all neatly placed on hangers.

'She didn't take many clothes?'

She shook her head. 'She was wearing her . . .' She choked on it.

'School uniform, I know. Take it easy, Jessie, Let's have a look here.'

Portia had one of those student's desks with a map of the world on it. A few text books were stacked on top of Europe and a pile of exercise books covered Australia. Jessie sank down on the bed and looked at me helplessly. 'Is there any hope?' she whispered.

'Sure.' I turned over the leaves of the books— domestic science; maths, social studies. They were neat and orderly. Another book had a clipping of Robert Redford pasted to the cover. On the first leaf 'Personal Development' was printed in bold letters. I showed it to Jessie.

'What's that?'

She shrugged. 'I'll just go and see if Jeff wants anything.' She started to get up but I waved her down.

'Hang on, won't be long.' I turned over the pages; there were poems and essays and questionnaires— all bland and almost impersonal. No outpourings of the heart here. Near the end of the filled-in pages there were marks on the back of one leaf. The scribble was in a different ink from the writing on the other side. I looked at it for a minute; Jessie looked too.

'Oh,' she said uninterestedly, 'I saw that. It's from a carbon paper put in the wrong way.'

'No, it isn't. Is Portia a left-hander, like you?'

'Yes.'

'Some left-handers can do mirror-writing automatically, without thinking. Can you?'

'I used to be able to, when I was a kid. I wouldn't have tried to in twenty-five ... a long time.'

I took the page over to the dressing table and looked at the image in the mirror. In an irregular hand, quite different from the rest of the writing in the book, was written: 'A woman at last! It was wonderful! I knew it would be. We both want more and more.'

Jessie stood beside me and stared at the mirror. Her shriek bounced off the walls. 'No! Oh God, no!'

Heavy footsteps shook the floor and Jeff Stevenson flung himself into the room; beer slopped from another can in his hand.

'What the hell ...'

Jessie leapt for him and clung. She buried her head in his shirt front and sobbed. Stevenson bullocked across the room, carrying her with him. He stared at the mirror and then at me. His high colour flamed even higher.

'Jesus, Jesus, what ... what does it mean?'

'I'd say it means she's got a boyfriend,' I said.

'Sixteen ...' Jessie sobbed.

'I thought she was seventeen,' I said.

'Only just.' Stevenson patted his wife's shoulder clumsily. I closed the book and put it back with the others.

'Let's go out and talk about it.' I virtually had to shepherd them out of the room and to the back of the house. Stevenson remembered his beer can and I re-possessed my red wine. We all sat down again and drank—except Jessie, who gripped her husband's knee.

'It helps,' I said. 'It supplies a reason. It gives us something, someone—to look for. Somebody must know who he is—a friend, someone in a coffee shop, a pub. Kids have got to go somewhere and there are people who know where they go. Cheer up.'

'I can't believe it,' Jessie said. 'I just can't believe it.'

'She *is* seventeen,' Stevenson muttered.

'But not to say a word. Not to bring him home, even. Oh, he must be *so* unsuitable.'

She was upset and confused and her mixed feelings were showing all too clearly—snobbery was strongly present along with the protectiveness and hurt.

I wrote the message in the exercise book in my notebook, working from memory. I tapped the contents of the folder into neatness. The Stevensons watched me.

'Now, does this give you any clues? Anything come to mind? Something you mightn't have thought of before?'

They shook their heads. I put the notebook away. 'Okay, I'll take it from here. Sorry, but I'll have to ask you for a retainer and some sort of letter of authority.'

Stevenson pulled down his waistcoat and sucked in his gut. 'Yes, of course. I'll fix it up. Ah, Jess, I could go a cup of coffee; you, Hardy?'

'No thanks.'

'I'll make some fresh, dear.' Jessie jumped up and headed towards a door behind the bar. Stevenson found his suit jacket hanging on a chair, dug into the breast pocket and pulled out a cheque book.

'Umm, Hardy, now you come to mention it, I think I do know something that might help. Five hundred do you for now?'

I nodded. He spread the cheque book on the bar and wrote.

'I'll get my secretary to knock up an authority. Put it in the post tomorrow. That do you?'

I nodded again and waited for whatever it was he was wanted to tell me. He ripped out the slip and handed it to me.

'Hardy, I . . . ah . . . didn't know what to make of this. I only heard it today and it didn't make any sense. But in view of what you found in that notebook . . . I didn't want to say anything in front of Jess.'

'About what?'

'Well, I put all sorts of feelers out, of course. People on the road come into the agency, you know. I've told them about our trouble. And this guy, he travels about a bit. He said he'd seen a girl who looked a bit like Portia over at a truck depot in Ryde. I don't know, it's probably nothing. But you know, the trucks go interstate from there . . .'

'What's the name of the place?'

He told me and I said I'd take a look there as well as re check with the girl's friends and teachers and do a thorough local snoop. I said I'd be in touch as soon as I needed anything.

'Or when you need more money,' he said.

'Yeah, well it would come to that if there's an interstate angle.'

'Interstate?' Jessie Stevenson came back into the room carrying a tray with a coffee pot, cups and sweet biscuits. Jeff's waistline was in for another hammering. 'What about interstate?'

'Nothing, love. Just talking. Goodnight, Hardy. I'll show you out.'

I nodded to Jessie's brave smile and followed him up the passage. Another too-strong handshake, and I was out in the cool evening air.

I drove to the trucking yard in Ryde, taking the long way home. The place was dark and quiet, and a fast food caravan was just closing down as I pulled up. The woman who ran the show was tired and impatient with my questions.

'Early night,' she said. 'D'you mind?'

'No. What about tomorrow?'

'Big night, open late. Trucks in 'n out till all hours.'

'Save me a hamburger.'

She grunted and slammed down the shutters.

I did the rounds the next day; Castlecrag isn't known for its low-life hang-outs, but I checked such places as seemed likely to be trysting points. No result. A check of the cab companies that do most of the area's business drew the same blank. I thought I should wait for Stevenson's letter of authority before tackling the school, but I phoned the homes of the kids on the list of Portia's friends and found one of them home with the flu. Her mother permitted me ten minutes with the kid after checking with Jessie.

The house was a sterile barn, too big for the woman and her two daughters who lived there. I gathered that Dad lived somewhere else. Tammy Martin's bedroom was pretty much like Portia's, except that she had more posters of younger guys—Michael Jackson, Christopher Atkins and the like. She sat up in bed with a glow of fever in her young cheeks and asked to see my gun.

'I don't carry a gun when I'm looking for a

seventeen-year-old girl,' I said.

'You never know.'

'What does that mean?'

'Nothin'. Just dialogue.'

She was bright and wanted to be helpful; she missed Portia and she phoo-phooed the idea that she had a boyfriend.

'I'd have known,' she said. 'We were like that.' She placed her index and second finger together, but she was wrong. I thanked her, said I hoped she'd get well soon, and left.

It was late afternoon when I got back to the trucking yard. The woman at the fast food bar looked tired already; she nodded sceptically at me when I waved to her. The yard was a big, flat expanse flanked by sheds like small aircraft hangars; a few prime movers and loaded semi-trailers stood casting ungainly shadows across the asphalt. A group of drivers leaned on a stack of wooden pallets; they yarned and smoked and looked incuriously at me as I walked across to the office, wedged between two high, wide loading bays. Before I reached the building, one of the drivers detached himself and strolled towards me.

'Help you, mate?'

I stopped. 'Well, I wanted to see the boss, foreman or whatever.' I could see a bespectacled man looking at us through a window in the office.

'Why?'

'I wanted to talk to the drivers.'

'You don't need to ask permission for that, mate. We're independents here. You want to talk, come on over and talk.' He jerked his head at the office. 'He's nobody.'

I followed him across to the pallets; there were four men there, all built big and wearing the dusty, greasy uniform of their calling. The man who had approached me simply joined the group and left me to sink or swim.

'G'day,' I said. 'Wondering if one of you blokes could help me.' I reached into my pocket and took out the most recent photograph of Portia—the one that showed her poised and confident in designer jeans, blouse and stylish jacket, standing in front of the Stevensons' house. I held up the picture. 'Seen her?'

One of the men, not the biggest but not the smallest, made a sound like a blocked drain clearing. He spat and reached for the front of my coat. I dropped the photograph.

'I've been waitin' for youse to turn up.' He pulled me close and swung a short, clubbing punch at my chin. I pulled free and back and made the punch miss. He swore and came at me again.

'Easy,' I said.

'Go on, Kenny,' one of the men urged, 'have a go!'

Kenny bustled forward and swung again. I took it on the shoulder and gave him a quick tap back. He ducked into it and was hit harder on the nose than I'd intended.

'Fuck you!' he roared. He came in again, swinging and lunging, and I gave ground until we were clear of the other men and I was sure of my footing. He squared up clumsily and I went under his lead and hammered his left side ribs. He almost overbalanced and I helped him down with a left hook under the ear. He sprawled on the dusty bitumen. The others moved threateningly but I pulled out my licence card and held it up.

'Hold on,' I said. 'This is a misunderstanding. Don't get excited.'

They hesitated and I crouched down beside Kenny who'd twisted his leg on his descent. I showed him the card.

'This is a legitimate investigation. What did you mean—about waiting for me?'

Kenny did some swearing then looked across at the office. 'That four-eyed nong in there tried to bribe me to say I'd seen the sheilah. Said someone'd be around askin'. I told him to get fucked and said I'd drop youse. You were a bit good, but.'

I took twenty dollars out of my wallet and put it on his chest. 'A misunderstanding, mate. What's his name?'

'Polly Adams—there 'e goes!'

A small man wearing a dust coat that flapped behind him, ran from the office between the loading bays. I took off like a sprinter from the blocks after him. He had a lead but he was no runner. I gained with every stride and the flapping coat caught on the wire that straggled from the cyclone fence where he had to make a turn. The coat ripped, he slowed down and I got my hand on his shoulder and ran him into the fence. he bounced off it and I pinned him back and held him there. We panted in each other other's face and I realised that I was crouching and holding him up on tip toe. I felt ashamed; he was about five foot three and weighed around eight stone. I let him down and took two fistfuls of the front of his dust coat.

'Just one question,' I said. 'Who told you to get a driver to lie to me?' I shook him and his head wobbled on his thin neck. His breath smelled of cigarettes—no wind.

'Silly bugger,' he gasped. 'He just hadda say it might've been her. He's off to the West in a coupla days. There was fifty bucks in it for him.'

'Who was he?'

'I dunno his name. Met him in the pub this morning. Well, I seen him there before once.'

'Description.'

'Big bloke, tall as you 'n heavier. Lot heavier. Red face, flash suit. Looked like a cop. I reckon he could be a cop.'

'Bullshit!' I let him go and he stayed there with his back against the wire; with his eyes and mouth open in fright and his torn coat flapping he looked like a scarecrow. I walked back to the yard. Kenny was leaning against the pallets with a cigarette in his mouth.

'You all right?' I said.

He nooded. I picked up the photograph and walked towards my car.

Five hours later I was in the car and parked fifty yards from the Stevenson's house in Cammeray. Jeff Stevenson came out, got into a light-blue Holden Statesman and drove away. I followed him. He drove fast but not very well and I had to cope with some ill-tempered drivers he created around him. He ploughed through to Lane Cove West and took a turn off the Epping Road down towards the river. The street was dark and quiet and the Statesman plunged down into a car park under a block of flats that hid behind high poplar trees discreetly illuminated from ground level.

I parked in the street, got a torch from the glove box and went down into the bunker. Each resident had two parking bays—one for a visitor. The Statesman was parked next to a new Honda Civic in Bay 36A. I prowled around the block of flats until I located the right entrance. The white stones crunched under my feet; my legs were brushed by ferns. The rents would be high. Flat 36A was occupied by Ann Stevens. I went back to my car, drove to the nearest liquor store for a half bottle of whisky and took up a position opposite the flats with the radio on softly and the bottle on my lap.

The Statesman roared up the ramp at a little past 2 a.m. I watched it out of sight, took one more swig on the bottle and drove carefully home.

I kept up a surveillance of the Stevensons for four days. Jeff Stevenson went to work in the mornings; Jessie slept late, moved like an automaton and went to her analyst. She drank gin in the afternoon. On the second night they went out to a restaurant; both drank a lot and Jessie almost raped him while they danced. The next night Stevenson arrived at Lane Cove West at midnight and Portia came out wearing a wig and a light coat with the collar turned up. They walked the streets, tightly locked together. She was tall and slim and her movements were graceful. She looked up at Jeff adoringly. I photographed them. I went through the rubbish bin for 36A and found a letter signed 'Jeff' and the foil from contraceptive pills.

Terry writhed in the bed. 'Oh God,' she said.

'I wore rubber gloves, don't worry.'

'It's not funny. What are you going to do?'

I thought of Jessie Stevenson's tight, strained face as she drove her car, of the boozy, dazed look she wore at 4 o'clock as she stood, aimless in her front garden. I'd watched her do that for an hour, wondering what she was doing until I saw the two girls in the school uniform turn into the street. Then she went inside. I remembered the way she looked at her husband.

'I don't know,' I said. 'What would you do?'

The Mongol Scroll

Dr Kangri hit the button on the slide projector and the image flashed up on the metre-square screen.

'Beautiful, is it not?' he said.

It was an oriental drawing showing a couple making love. They were both wearing robes and had painted faces and their hair tied back in severe knots. They were smiling; the man had a big erection and the woman had small, pointed breasts. The erection was between the breasts and they both seemed pretty pleased about it. The colours were brilliant blues, reds and yellows and the lovers were on a thin mat in a sparsely furnished room that seemed to be full of sunlight.

'Yes,' I said. 'Beautiful's the word.'

He showed the next slide and the next, and half a dozen more. They were all in the same mood and communicated the same feeling: extreme pleasure in leisurely, inventive sex. My mouth was a bit dry when he turned the projector off; I could have managed to look at a few more without too much trouble.

He tidied the slides away and moved the projector aside. Then he sat down behind the big desk in the study crammed with books and paintings and scrolls and I turned my chair around away from the screen and faced him.

'They are very fine,' he said, 'but nothing compared to the impact of the scroll itself.'

'The subject's the same all through?'

He smiled. Dr Kangri was a small, smooth-faced man in his late fifties. To judge from his house in Vaucluse, the Jaguar in the garage, the furnishings and the art work, his assets would have been in the early millions. 'Erotic, you mean? Yes, very, Splendidly so and a very rare scroll. Unique.'

'Worth?'

He shrugged, moving his shoulders fluidly inside his silk shirt. He seemed to have the movements of a much younger man. *Yoga*? I thought.

'Who can say? Priceless.'

'I'm sorry to be crude about it, doctor. But I need a price, so will the insurance people. You must have paid . . .'

A few lines of annoyance appeared on the smooth, brown skin and then vanished as if dismissed by an act of will. 'It is not insured, Mr Hardy. I paid; yes, indeed I paid, but in favours you understand. Services, not cash.'

I got out a notebook because it looks efficient and can sometimes be useful. I wrote 'Chinese scroll' and put a question mark beside a dollar sign. Then I scratched the words out because Kangri proceeded to tell me that it wasn't a Chinese scroll but a Tibetan scroll in a Mongol style. The scroll was about two metres long and forty centimetres wide; and had thirty-seven sections, each showing an erotic scene. Apparently the scroll was like the Chinese 'Pillow books' which were presented to newly weds to give them the right idea and put them in the mood. 'Almost all Tibetan art is religious,' Kangri told me. 'This scroll is a rare exception.'

It sounded like a nice exception to me. 'Old?'

'Fifteenth century. Never before reproduced, hardly known. My edition will make big waves.'

It was an oddly contemporary expression to come

from such a traditional-seeming man. I doubted whether he knew that it was contemporary. I nodded and listened while he told me that he was planning a lavish book, reproducing the scroll along with a scholarly essay and notes by himself. The slides had come his way ten years before, and the work of acquiring the scroll itself and doing the scholarly investigation and occupied him for twenty years.

'When did you get the scroll?' I asked.

'One month ago. I thought about it for twenty years and had it for a mere thirty days.'

Unique or not, the procedure's much the same when investigating the nicking of something. Where was it kept? When did you last see it? Who knew it was there? Kangri told me he'd kept the scroll in a locked cupboard in the study and he showed me the broken lock. He'd last looked at his treasure four days before and only his daughter, his housekeeper and an academic named Dr Susan Caswell knew where it was kept. I looked around the over-stocked but tidy room, noted the labels on pots and the classification numbers on the spines of the books.

'Was anything else taken?'

'Yes, many things—other scrolls, books, ornaments. Some of value, others not. All insured. A few things were broken, but I have had the study cleaned. I ruminated for several days before taking this action.'

'I'll have to talk to these people.'

He nodded. 'Certainly, but Dr Caswell left Australia for Tibet a week ago on sabbatical leave. Mrs Tsang, my housekeeper, is at your disposal. My daughter may be a little hard to locate, but I assume you have ways of doing that.'

'Yes. Before we get into that, could you tell me why you called me in on this? I mean, I haven't got any connections with the ...'

He smiled again and the skin hardly crinkled. 'You were going to say "Chinese community" although you know that I am a Tibetan. It's very difficult for you. Well, Mr Hardy. I made some enquiries when this matter arose. I needed someone discreet, of course, and you come highly commended on that score. But I also learned that you fought against the Chinese communists in Malaya.'

'Yes, well ...'

'The only successful anti-guerilla campaign in history. I wish my poor country had had such allies. You know of the subjugation of Tibet by China?'

I knew that the Dalai Lama wasn't top dog there anymore and that the Chinese didn't have any trouble going up mountains from the Tibetan side, but my knowledge ended about there. Kangri took silence for assent and went on, 'I left my country in 1950 when the conquest began. I went to the United States to study and to go into business.'

'What business was that?' I had the notebook at the ready.

'Importing art objects from my country and India. I prospered, then I came here where I have continued to prosper. My country has been forgotten, overlooked. It is an anachronism, an irrelevance. My edition of the scroll will perhaps correct that. It will show that Tibet had a rich, humanistic culture, that it was not just a society of peasants and priests.'

I had already classified the good doctor as a pretty shrewd number. I had the feeling that his business might have involved some corner-cutting and I'd have bet that his doctorate wasn't from Harvard. But all the signs were that he could write a good cheque; and if he wanted to think I'd idealistically thrown my young body into the fray against the communistic menace, instead of just wanting to get out of Australia and having the sense to do what I was told for a while, who was I to disillusion him?

'Does anyone else know you have the scroll? I mean, other Tibetans, scholars?'

'No. Only the people I have mentioned. My daughter would not be interested enough to tell anyone. Mrs Tsang is totally discreet. Dr Caswell would realise the penalties of any publicity.'

'Penalties?'

'Obvious, surely. This is a highly erotic work. The newspapers would fall on it as a spicy story. My edition would be seen in the worst possible light. I shudder at the thought.'

I could see his point; headlines like 'Sex Scroll Stolen' wouldn't strike the right scholarly note. I had a lot of questions, but some of them I could put to other people. I closed the notebook and stood up.

'Just one question, Dr Kangri; don't be insulted. As your agent I'm protected if I get hold of the scroll only if it's your property. Is it?'

'Yes, in every sense.'

'Good. Perhaps you could give me a list of places that would be interested in such things—dealers, collectors.'

'I'm afraid not. You're slipping into the same mistake, Mr Hardy, assuming I am part of some sort of community in this city. There is no Tibetan community in Sydney. I know of no ... shop that would have any knowledge of such a scroll as this.'

'If some dealer in oriental things got hold of it would its value be immediately apparent?'

'Not necessarily. I can't bear to think of such a thing.'

'I'll have to think of it then. Could I see your housekeeper?'

'Of course.' He opened a drawer in the desk, took

out a cheque book and looked at me enquiringly.

'A hundred and twenty-five dollars a day and expenses,' I said. 'Two days fee in advance if that's convenient.'

He wrote and handed me the cheque. He stood up with another of those easy, youthful movements and went around the desk. 'I'll send Mrs Tsang in here. I'm afraid I have an appointment now, so I will hope to get a report from you soon, Mr Hardy. You appreciate that I am very distressed over this, and I am placing all my hopes in you.'

It was just as well he told me. For all the emotion he displayed we could have been talking about a lost sock. We nodded inscrutably at each other and he went out. I wondered if I should go behind the desk but I decided not to. I perched on the edge of it instead. Nice desk, good wood, carved. Nice carpet; good bookshelves; nice cupboard, pity about the smashed lock. Pity about the priceless scroll too.

The woman who knocked at the door was medium-sized with black hair drawn tightly back and a very erect carriage. She stood straight and still with her knuckles just an inch from the door jamb. I felt awkward in the oppressively scholarly room and even more so now summoning forward someone who lived in the house. I tried a smile and a wave.

'Come in, Mrs Tsang, come in.' I sounded like a housemaster or what I imagined a housemaster sounded like—we didn't have them at Maroubra High. She walked in and stood in front of me. I was going to have to go the whole hog.

'Please sit down.' She sat in the chair I'd vacated, still stiff and straight in her dark plain dress and sensible shoes. Like Dr Kangri she had a smooth brown face and she gave off an air of having lived on this earth for a good spell rather than looking old. Her mouth was thin and straight, her slanted black eyes were still; as Kangri had seemed to minimise emotion she minimised movement.

'You know why I'm here, Mrs Tsang?'

'Yes, sir.'

Sir, maybe I'd got the housemaster note right after all.

'Can you help me?'

She shook her head.

'Were you in the house when the study was . . . disturbed?'

'Some of the time, not all. I went shopping. The house was not always attended.'

'Did you set the alarm system?' As a matter of professional habit I'd noticed that the house had a thorough, if not very modern, set of door and window alarms.

'Yes, sir; but the alarm, it does not always work. Dr Kangri has said that the system provides a deterrent and that is enough.'

She said this, one of the dopiest things it's possible to say in Sydney where there's a burglary every five minutes, as if it was a revered, unquestionable statement.

'Did you come into this room that day?'

'No, sir. I dust the room once a week, that is all. I did not come in here until Dr Kangri cried out that the scroll had gone.' She paused as if for breath. 'And I have not been in since, until this time.' It sounded pat, rehearsed, but she had a strange lilt in her voice and it was hard to tell—she might have sounded like that when buying cabbages.

I ran through the usual questions: see anything unusual that day? No. Any deliveries to the house? No. Gas, phone, electricity men? No. Then I gave her one that made her blink.

'Where is Dr Kangri's wife?'

Blink. 'She died several years ago.'

I felt that I was getting better at reading her and I guessed that Kangri's widowhood didn't displease her. Then the stillness came over her again and she didn't blink when I asked her where I might find the good doctor's daughter and what her name was.

'May Kangri,' she said evenly. 'She left an address recently for her cheques to be sent to.'

'Cheques?'

'Her father sends her a cheque each month—it is almost their only form of commmunication.'

Something about the way she spoke made me feel as if I'd been dismissed. I got off the desk and put the trusty notebook in my jacket pocket. I was wearing a cord jacket with patch pockets. For once, I even had leather shoes on and pants with a crease. Mrs Tsang ushered me out of the study and closed the door firmly behind us. We went down a passage decked out with things that looked Chinese to me but probably weren't. The decor of the sitting room she left me in while she got the address looked Indian but it was probably Nepalese.

She came back quickly and handed me a folded piece of paper. I left the house through one of the doors guarded by a burglar alarm that didn't work. The Jag had gone. I wondered if *its* alarm worked.

I couldn't say I felt very hopeful as I went down the path towards the street where I'd left my car. Dr Kangri was like a cryptic crossword with not enough clues, and Mrs Tsang, even if she hadn't told me all she knew, looked like she could stand a few weeks of torture without squealing. At the gate, I turned and looked back at the house; it was one of those big, solid places with two or three different levels and interesting angles. There were vines growing over some of the white painted brickwork and a big, curved window was reflecting the late afternoon sun. There was not a single Oriental touch on the outside and hardly an Occidental one inside.

With a thick-tipped pen Mrs Tsang had written 48 Royal Street, Darlinghurst. It was a long step from the Kangri mansion with the vines and the park just across the way, and the glittering water beyond the trees and grass. As always when I drive around Sydney, I left the water with some reluctance. There's nothing much to be said for driving into Darlinghurst at 5 o'clock on a Thursday afternoon, especially since they've blocked off all the streets so that you can't get within three blocks of where you want to go. I parked near one of the barriers and walked through a set of narrow lanes to Royal Street. Number 48 was in the middle of a narrow terrace presenting a flat, blank face to the street. It had the standard bars on the windows and the standard bluestone front step worn concave by more than a hundred years of feet.

I knocked and waited. After a while a young girl in a man's singlet came to the door and stood there, blinking at the fading light and rubbing her eyes.

'I'm looking for May Kangri.'

'Who the fuck is it?' A man's voice rumbled in the hall behind her. She didn't look at me or turn to answer; she just spoke into the void above my head.

'Some straight lookin' for May.'

'Tell him to piss off.'

'Piss . . .,' she began, but I shouldered her aside and went through the door. The passage was dark but I could see a large shape at the end of it; as I came closer to the shape I began to smell it.

'You tell me to piss off,' I said. 'Why don't you try being polite? You might like it.'

He was short and burly with massive stubby arms—not someone to wrestle with. 'May Kangri; this is the last address I've got for her and it's recent.'

He grunted and tried to kick me in the stomach, I leaned against the wall to make him miss and then felt the breath go out of me and a pain begin in my foot and travel up my leg. He'd turned the missed kick into a stomp faster than the eye could see. I backed off and kept by the wall. He came after me in a fast shuffle and I didn't know whether to watch his hands or his feet. He lowered his head as if he might try some butting as well and that was a mistake; I used my much longer reach to get a fistful of his thick greasy hair. I yanked it like pulling weeds and he squealed and flailed his club-like arms. I kept clear and bore down hard; it would have scalped him if he hadn't gone down with the pressure. I got behind him, laced my fingers into the hair and bent him back in a kneeling position so that my knee dug in half way down his spine. I dug in hard and he screamed.

'Come here!' The girl jumped as I snapped at her: she looked as if she'd been about to run out the door. 'Your friend's in pain,' I said. 'Where's May Kangri?'

'Heavy,' she said.

The man on his knees spoke in a voice that sounded like heart-broken sobbing. 'She's at Rushcutters Bay, on a fuckin' boat. Let the fuck go.'

'Where at Rushcutters Bay?'

'Marina, next to the fuckin' yacht squadron.'

'Name of boat?' I eased back on the knee.

'Poppie, Pansy, somethin' like that. Shit!'

'When did she go aboard, Captain?'

'Yes'd'day.'

I let go the hair and pushed him down flat on his face. He lay there gasping and I stepped over him and round the girl. She was still blinking as if she'd stepped out into the noon sun.

'Excuse me,' I opened the door. 'Polite, see? I'm

sure your friend could get the hang of it if he tried.'

'Piss off,' she said.

'What's the matter with you people? Why're you so bloody aggressive?'

She sniggered. 'Wait'll you meet May.' Then she slammed the door in my face.

Back to the water I need never have left had I only known. That's the story of a private eye's life; as often as not the trail ends where it began, that's when there turns out to be a trail at all. This sort of thinking occupied me on the trip to Rushcutters Bay and it either made me tired or made me realise that I was tired already. It had been a week of long drives and late nights on matters personal and professional, and if I'd been Nero Wolf or Whimsey or someone like that I wouldn't have taken Kangri's job on grounds of exhaustion. But I needed the money.

It was close to 7 o'clock when I arrived, the butt end of a mild March day, and the light was almost spent. Beyond the water the city skyscape rose up, jagged-shaped and erratically lit. A half-turn and I could see clear across the water to North Sydney.

It's a wonder there isn't more theft, vandalism and arson on tied-up boats because the security at the average marina is lousy. There was virtually none at Rushcutters Bay. The marina was flanked by closed shops that sold nautical gear, a clubhouse and a slipway with boats drawn up high and dry for servicing or whatever they call it. A weatherbeaten old pipe-smoker leaning against the timber office at the end of the wharf took an uninterested look at me as I stepped over the loose chain and headed for the boats. Maybe it was the patch-pocket jacket that did the trick.

There was only just enough light to read names

by; some I had to squint at, a few I had to guess at. There was no *Pansy* but a *Tall Poppy* was bobbing near the end of the better lit stretch of wharf—the part which provided light, water, power and would get cable TV when it came.

It was a sleek white boat with two masts, furled sails and a lot of glass and brass and pale yellow rope scattered about. I went to the edge of the planking and called down, feeling slightly silly at talking loudly to a boat. A light came on near the stern and I heard a scuffling noise and a few muffled giggles. A woman's head appeared through a hole in the deck followed by her upper body and legs. She stood up against the night sky and looked to be about seven feet tall. It was an illusion; as she moved closer I could see that she was only six feet tall—long and willowy with cropped dark hair. She was naked apart from a few gold chains around her neck; the chains glinted in the marina lights and her skin, which was about the same colour, gleamed.

'Yes?' she said.

'Are you May Kangri?'

'Yes. Who're you?'

'My name's Hardy, I'm a private detective, working for your father.'

She was close now, just a few feet below me on the deck; her body was about perfect as six foot, golden female bodies go. She had the slightly flat face of her father but I wouldn't have taken many points off for that.

'Who told you I was here?' Her voice was without warmth, almost hostile.

'The guy at Royal Street.'

'Fuck him.'

'Don't blame him. He didn't want to tell me, I had to persuade him.'

That seemed to interest her; she looked up and her

breasts moved and the movement rippled down her body. I tried to keep from gaping.

'You persuaded him. Did you use a gun?'

'No. I pulled his hair a little.'

She laughed, again without warmth but even she couldn't manage to laugh with hostility. A voice called from behind her, a female voice, American.

'May, who is it, honey?'

'A man,' May Kangri said.

Another head poked up, a blonde one this time, and it was followed by a body wrapped in a towelling dressing gown. The woman was about twice May Kangri's age—which I guessed to be middle-twenties—and what she lacked in beauty she made up in aggression. She marched forward, elbowed the girl aside and glared up at me.

'What d'you want, mister?'

The naked, golden body moved, swivelled and one hand came crashing against the side of the blonde woman's head; she staggered and the combination followed—a sweeping leg that scythed her down like wheat and crashed her to the deck. She lay in a crumpled heap and May Kangri delivered a modest kick to her exposed backside.

'Don't be bossy with me, Candy. I won't take it.'

Candy got up stiffly; tears were running down her swollen face and she limped off towards the hatch. The action had put a light film of sweat on the golden skin and I was finding it hard to keep my professional detachment. She smiled up at me— white teeth in a flat, brown face. I'd rather have gone up against the guy in Royal Street again.

'What's Daddy's problem?'

'Why don't you put some clothes on and we can have a talk?'

'I'm not wearing any clothes today. Talk quick, I'm easily bored.'

'Something valuable's been stolen from your father's house—a scroll. Do you know anything about it?'

'That ancient, creepy shit? No, what would I know about it?'

The interview wasn't turning out to be one of my best. I felt like a combination of perv and headshrinker. I went direct. 'You seem to be a forthright young woman, Miss Kangri. You didn't pinch your father's scroll either for money or to rub his nose in the shit?'

She gave the laugh again, this time with a bit of contempt in it. I felt pretty sure she'd be good at contempt. 'No, I didn't. I don't need money. Candy's loaded and I'm going for a trip around the world with her on the yacht. We're off tomorrow. Wanna come?'

I grinned, shook my head and backed off. She turned around and sauntered off towards the stern; she moved well, like her Dad. Somehow I didn't think that stealing the scroll would be her style of spite—she'd be more likely to burn the house down.

That left me with no obvious leads and the slightly defeated feeling that goes with that situation. My hand was greasy from contact with the Darlinghurst stomper and I walked down a few steps from one of the stagings on the marina and had a wash. My face was hot and I dabbed it with the cool salt water. It was dark now and cool with a nice breeze coming off the water, but the park at Rushcutters Bay is no place for a clean living man to hang around in at night. I drove down New South Head Road, ate some fish somewhere, drank a fair bit of white wine and went home to sleep on it.

In the morning the memory of May Kangri's exotic body had faded and the need to earn the figures written on Dr Kangri's cheque asserted itself. The job looked routine again; I rang a few people and found out the names and addresses of some establishments that dealt in rare Oriental items. Most of these places had spotless reputations, but a few didn't. I drove and walked, heard eastern chimes ring when I pushed open doors and looked into black slanted eyes until I was sick of them. I encountered universal politeness and universal ignorance.

After two full days on the job I'd earned the advance fee but not a cent more and didn't look like earning it. I was sitting at home reading *Unreliable Memoirs* when the phone rang. It was Mrs Tsang inviting me out to Vaucluse to tell me things about the Mongol scroll that she hadn't told me before.

She was waiting for me by the front gate. I pulled up outside the house next door which gave me a fair walk back to where she stood. She was wearing the same dark dress and had a light shawl around her shoulders.

'Come this way,' she whispered, 'to my flat.'

We walked on the grass towards a narrow path leading to the dark side of the house.

'Is the doctor home, Mrs Tsang?'

'Yes, perhaps you will want to see him but I must speak to you first.'

The path ended at a set of wooden steps with a glass panelled door at the top. She went ahead of me into a narrow kitchen that faced the wall of the next house; that left space for a nice patch of garden and a good glimpse of the night sky. Through the kitchen and into a sitting room with cane furniture. The eastern look was dominant as in the main part of Kangri's house but there were counter-influences—framed photographs with Western faces in them and Australian books and magazines.

'Please sit down, Mr Hardy. Would you care for tea?'

'No thank you, Mrs Tsang. What do you have to tell me?'

It came out hesitantly, but coherently. Mrs Tsang had taken the scroll herself and faked the disturbance of the study. She spoke very softly and I had to lean forward from my chair to hear her.

'Like Dr Kangri, I am Tibetan,' she said. 'But unlike him I am a religious person. Do you know anything of the religion of my country, Mr Hardy?'

I had to admit that I didn't.

'It is very ancient and beautiful. It is a Buddhist religion but with many influences from the old religion of Tibet—many wonderful rituals and prayers.'

'Uh huh.'

'You are a non-believer, like most Australians. A materialist. It is very sad. Tibetan culture and religion are synomymous, Mr Hardy.'

'What about the scroll?'

'It cannot possibly be genuine,' she said fiercely. 'It is impossible that the monks can have produced such a thing. It is counter to all teachings, all beliefs.'

'Dr Kangri believes it to be genuine.'

'He is mistaken.' She drew a breath. 'I took the scroll when I could see what he was planning—a book that would bring my religion into the greatest questioning, the greatest disrepute. There are scholars who could prove that it is a fake. Dr Kangri would not consult them.' She leaned back on her chair, took a handkerchief from her sleeve and patted her moist forehead.

'It's his property, Mrs Tsang, you must return it.'

Her brown face was composed again but there was

a look of fatigue in the composure. 'It is not his property,' she said softly. 'He acquired it by underhand means. But that is not important. I cannot return it, Mr Hardy. It has been stolen from me in turn.'

'Who by?'

'My son, my only child.'

Children again, only children, tearing at their parents as if to punish them for something. Mrs Tsang showed me the photograph of Henry, her son, and his father. The father was Australian—long faced and jawed, squint-eyed, sandy-haired, strong on character, short on sense of humour perhaps. The son favoured him; the dark eyes hardly slanted and the jutting Scots physiognomy dominated over the Tibetan flatness.

Mrs Tsang has met and married Kevin Anderson in Burma after the war. Anderson had served in the country, and had gone back there after demobilisation to work as a plantation manager. He was killed in an accident on the plantation not long after Henry was born. She heard of Dr Kangri's researches through her contacts with Tibetan priests and joined his household in the United States. The Immigration Department had put no obstacles in her way when Kangri had transplanted to Australia.

'Henry is not a good man. He has had a lot of trouble with the police.'

'What name does he go by?'

'I hardly know. I do not use my married name because it does not please me. Henry would use whatever name suited him, for whatever his purpose might be.'

'What purposes does he have?'

She closed her eyes and didn't answer. I was about to ask the question again when she opened her eyes and sat up straight.

'Evil ones. I had the scroll here. He came, looking for money as he often did. He took it. I went to see him to ask for it back and he laughed at me. I stole, and he thought it funny.'

'Did he say why he took it?'

She shook her head. 'I was not sure of this when you were here before. I suspected. But now I know it. Dr Kangri is blind to the truth but he is a clever man. He chose you because he believed you could be trusted. I am following him. Will you go to Henry and recover the scroll . . . and not harm my son?'

It was a tallish order, but Mrs Tsang was a shrewdie too. She'd worked it out that Kangri wouldn't prosecute Henry for the same reasons as he didn't want the theft publicised. She wanted Henry in the clear to go on making her life a misery. If Kangri gave her the sack, so be it. In the face of such calculation and forbearance, what could I do? I gave my word not to hurt Henry if it was humanly possible and she told me where to find him.

I left her in her kitchen making tea and possibly thinking how far off Nirvana was for Henry. The address she'd given me was in Petersham. I went there via home where I picked up some burglary tools and my .38 police special. I hadn't promised not to hurt Henry if he was trying to hurt me.

Terminal Street runs along the railway line and if you had one of the houses that sat right on the street with no front garden you had trouble, with or without double glazing. The house Mrs Tsang had nominated was one of those, a shabby building at the wrong end of the terrace—the end where the railway was closest and the factory threw the longest shadow. The house was dark in the front rooms and hall; I went around to the lane at the back, hoisted myself up on the fence and peered into a pocket-handkerchief backyard and at the crumbling back of what looked to be a totally dark, empty house.

I was contemplating the crime of break and enter when a light came on inside. I dropped back into the lane and raced around to the street. The front door of the house stood open and there was a station wagon outside on the wrong side of the street with the kerbside door open and the motor running. I heard feet pounding the stairs inside the house and saw more lights go on inside. Then a shouted curse. I scooted across to my car on the other side of the street, climbed in and hunched down to steering wheel level.

The man who ran out of the house slamming the door and hurling himself into the car was Henry Tsang-Anderson. He was taller than I thought he'd be and pretty fit to judge by his flowing movements. He was carrying a briefcase which he tossed over the back before slamming the car into gear. He roared off towards Lewisham and I started my motor and followed, not putting on my lights until he'd made his first turn.

The station wagon was an old Holden, not a good road holder and not hard to keep in sight. I kept my Falcon in the classical position, one back and not trapped on either side, and tooled along behind him. He picked up the Hume Highway and followed it for long enough to make me worry about going to Melbourne, but he swung off in Chullora and drove into the tight web of streets near the railway workshops. The traffic was almost non-existent and I had to keep well back. He stopped and I drove past keeping my head to the front and nearly displacing my eyeballs with sideways looks.

The Holden was parked outside a low, iron roofed, concrete workshop carrying a sign, hand-painted on a sheet of tin, that read TOP SPOT PRINTING. I parked fifty metres up the street and came back with the .38 in my waistband and a slowly dawning idea of what was happening. It seemed to be my night for creeping around buildings; I stayed in the shadows and worked my way to the back of the workshop. It was a run-down place with grass sprouting from the foundations and broken windows sealed up with wood and tin. At the back I stacked a couple of boxes on top of a pile of pallets and looked through a high window.

There were three men in the single room, one working at an offset press, another at a heavy-duty guillotine and stapler and Henry was unfolding boxes, stacking the product into them and sealing them with heavy tape. The briefcase he'd brought from Petersham was standing on the floor near him—he glanced down at it from time to time and so did the tall, skinny guy at the press.

The trimmer and stapler was a freckled redhead, young and nervous-looking. He worked fast until he'd got ahead of the pages being fed to him, stopped, and lit a cigarette. Henry shouted something and the kid snarled back and marched over to the rear door about a metre from where I was standing. I dropped down and went around the nearest corner. Light flooded out through the open door and the kid puffed his cigarette angrily. He flipped the butt out and I heard a voice say 'Leave it open.'

He did and that suited me because I sneaked back to the doorway and could hear most of what was said inside. After the noise of printing and packing stopped, they fell to arguing about money. The youthful voice I took to be the redhead's; it must have been Henry who spoke next because he said he'd gone and got the bloody money, hadn't he?

The skinny guy said what was going to happen to the fuckin' painting and Henry said that was his business and he was taking the risks by keeping it at his place.

The redhead said: 'Well, let's have some bloody cash now and you'd better come up with some more.'

Henry said not to threaten him and the other guy told them both to shut up. I heard the sound of money slapping down on a table and some quiet counting.

'That's for starters,' Henry said. 'There's plenty more to come. We'll make the first delivery tomorrow. I want you both here at 10 o'clock with your cars. And don't get on the piss tonight.'

There was some grumbling and I had to nick around the corner again as one of them slammed and locked the back door. The lights went out and I heard three motors start and the cars drive away. The street was quiet and not particularly well lit. There were a number of small factories, vacant lots and only a few houses some distance from the print shop. A light, curiosity-deterring rain started to fall. Boldness seemed to be indicated; I put my car in front of the building, got out the tools and broke in at the back. I turned on the lights and opened the front door. Nothing stirred in the street.

The photographic plates were set up on the press. They showed the thirty-seven sections of the scroll in full colour and slightly muzzy detail. A drawer in a desk contained slides and other photographic preparations that preceded the making of the plates. I broke open one of the eight boxes and took a look at the result of all this activity. It was a fifty-page stapled book, printed on rough paper and entitled *Tibetan Love Positions*. The colour was variable; the most explicit of the sections had been crudely reproduced and touched up to form the cover of the book. Even in this shoddy form the beauty of the drawings was remarkable and the sexual acts shown were varied without being perverse or contorted. The pleasure on the faces of the participants hit you in the eye and made the crude captions lettered in underneath all the more offensive.

I took the plates out of the press, collected all the stuff from the drawer—including a copy of the book that hadn't had the captions stripped in—and the eight boxes and stowed the lot in the car. I turned off the lights, closed the front door and drove away.

On the drive back to Petersham I went carefully on the wet roads and wondered if Henry had taken his own advice and settled down for a quiet, sober night. It looked that way. The Holden was parked neatly in front of the house and all the lights were out bar one in the toilet at the back. No music, no dogs, no television. I climbed over the back fence and went in through the back door which had a light lock that took me less than a minute to open.

The house was shabby inside and very untidy. It looked as if renovations had started and stopped; the bedroom downstairs was crammed with timber and had no floorboards. The other rooms weren't much better. The stairs were sound though, and I picked my way up them using a thin torch beam to negotiate the bends. Henry was in the front room asleep all alone in a double bed. He lay on his back and snored; lank dark hair fell forward on his face which was fatter than in the photograph I had seen.

I sat on the edge of the bed, put the muzzle of the .38 in his mouth and rapped hard against one of his back teeth. He jerked awake and I dug the gun in between his front teeth and upper lip. His eyes were wide in shock. I kept the gun wedged firmly in and worked the slide to cock it. The sound in the quiet room was like a door falling in. It must have sounded even worse to Henry.

'Where's the scroll, Henry? I'll take this out to let you tell me. If you don't I'll put it back and when the first train goes by you get a bullet going upwards.' A train rumbled past; the house shook and rattled. I grinned at Henry. 'You get the idea?'

He nodded and terror shone from his eyes.

'Okay. Make it quick, you get one chance.' I took the gun out and saliva ran down from his mouth. I held the small dark hole level with his right eye.

'Under the bed,' he said shakily, 'Box...'

'Get it!'

I eased back, and he came up trembling and having difficulty moving his limbs in the right sequence. I followed him with the gun like a movie camera panning as he rolled forward and scrabbled under the bed. He pulled up with a heavy metal box with a hinged lid. I gestured for him to open it; he put his hand inside the neck of his T-shirt and drew up a small key on a chain. The fingers holding the key shook and he scratched around the lock before he got it open and and took out the scroll. It looked like the real thing—right dimensions, light fabric rolled around a slender piece of wood. I nodded and he put it back in the box which I tucked under my arm.

'Who're you? You want bread?'

I shook my head. 'No questions, Henry. No answers.'

He lay back on the bed and didn't show any signs of getting braver. Maybe he could reconcile himself to losing the scroll so I thought I should tell him just how bad things were.

'I've got the books too,' I said, 'and the plates and the negs.'

There was a new level of fright in the dark eyes now.

'Jesus,' he said, 'I've been paid... I paid out...'

I smiled at him. 'I know you did, mate. I was there. I was sorry to see you do that.'

'They'll kill me.'

'I suggest you take a trip, Henry. No one's going to miss you.' I levelled the gun at his chest and got off the bed. 'Roll over on your front and stay there until you hear the next train. That way you can think about your next move and I won't have to shoot you.'

Down the stairs and out the front door. A train rushed past as I made the turn out of Terminal Street. It was well after midnight but it's never too late for good news. I rang Kangri's number and he answered, sounding strained and tired.

'I'm sorry to call so late.'

'It's all right, Mr Hardy. I cannot sleep.'

'You can now, I've got the scroll.'

He made a yipping sound and I would have liked to have seen his face. There might even have been a smile on it. I drove out to Vaucluse through the drizzle and ran the Falcon up the drive and in beside the Jag. Kangri was there waiting for me, wearing his suit. Mrs Tsang was there too, in a dressing gown. I managed to give her an encouraging nod when Kangri was examining the scroll.

'Wonderful, Mr Hardy. Undamaged. Wonderful. Thank you. A bonus, most certainly.'

I said a bonus would be nice and dragged out the box I'd opened. I handed him one of the books.

'My God,' he said, 'Appalling. Who...?'

I shook my head. 'Sources, Dr Kangri. Don't ask.' I gave him the plates and other stuff.

'The boil is lanced, then?' he said.

'Yeah.' I got out the other boxes and stacked them by a wall.

'I will get you a cheque.' He rushed off towards the house.

Mrs Tsang wrapped her elaborately embroidered dressing gown tightly around her and looked up at me.

'Henry?'

I nodded. 'He's okay, untouched. But he's in big trouble with his partners. I think he'll be going away for a while.'

Kangri came back and handed me a cheque. He was almost bubbling and he forgot himself enough to put his arm around Mrs Tsang as he spoke to her.

'We will burn this rubbish, eh, Mrs Tsang?'

'Yes,' she said.

I said goodnight and backed out leaving them standing close together, caught in my headlights. A gilt dragon coiled around Mrs Tsang's slim body.

Dr Kangri's bonus was pretty quickly spent and when his book came out it was in a limited edition and cost a thousand bucks a copy. But I've still got the uncaptioned copy of *Tibetan Love Positions* —it's one of my more stimulating souvenirs.

The Mae West Scam

Mr Joseph Thackeray was a literary agent. That made both of us agents, me being a private enquiry ditto. The first thing Mr Thackeray did after informing me of his profession and seating his narrow frame in one of the sagging chairs in my office, was ask me how much I charged.

'One hundred and twenty-five dollars a day plus expenses.' I said. 'How about you?'

He looked annoyed. 'Ten per cent of my client's earnings.'

'Handy if you've got David Williamson—have you?'

He looked still more annoyed. 'No, but I've got Carla Cummings, at least for now. Are you always this flippant, Mr Hardy?'

'Yeah, always, don't tell me you take agenting seriously?'

His prim little mouth pursed up, and he brushed wispy hair back from his high forehead. The narrow shoulders and the silly bow tie made him look like a lightweight but he had an incongruously deep and forceful voice. I've got better shoulders and don't wear bow ties; my voice isn't much but then, I do most of my agenting on the street rather than on the phone.

'I certainly do,' the strong voice from the weak face said. 'I consider myself a facilitator of literature.'

'At ten per cent.'

He drew in a deep breath, which made his Adam's apply move in his scrawny neck but made his voice more resonant. 'I'll persist because I'm told you're good at this sort of thing. Talented, someone said; although I can't think how the word applies.'

'Let's hope you will see when we're through. You've got a problem with Carla Cummings?'

'I can see you listen when you're being spoken to, that's good. Yes, a problem.'

It was the first approving word he'd spoken; we were getting along famously already. I leaned back in my sagging chair and let him tell it.

Carla Cummings was a country girl, born in Dubbo, who'd worked as a nurse and written thirty novels before her thirty-first was published. She was only thirty herself at the time, so she'd averaged better than three unpublished novels per year for ten years. *The Crying Gulls* made it all worthwhile. The book was a three-generation family saga set on the north coast of New South Wales. According to Cummings's own account in the many interviews she gave after the paperback rights were sold for two million dollars, she'd constructed the book to make it ideal for abridgement, extraction and serialisation. It was abridged, extracted and serialised everywhere, and the hard cover edition sold out and was reprinted three times. It was a million dollar movie property, and heartily loathed by every reviewer who touched it.

'She hasn't written a word since she finished *Gulls*,' Thackeray said.

'Can't see what I can do about writer's block.'

'That's only part of the problem. She's drinking, she's neurotic, gambling, falling out with everyone.'

'With you?'

'Especially with me.'

'You're worried about your ten per cent.'

He sighed. 'I have to assume that this aggression, this ... boorishness is your stock in trade. Yes, I'm concerned about my income and my reputation both—I assume you're concerned about yours?'

'Yeah. Fair enough, Mr Thackeray, didn't mean to ride you. What's troubling her? Not money? Not the bad reviews?'

He laughed a laugh that would have sounded good over the phone, rich and amused. 'I doubt if she read them. She was such a carefree creature—scatter-brained you'd have said. She was the easiest of clients.'

'Meaning what?'

'Oh, she'd talk to anyone, wouldn't haggle about every little detail—not like some of them.'

The few writers I knew were drunks and fragile egotists; it was refreshing to hear about a carefree one.

'Is she a good writer?' I asked.

Thackeray plucked at his bow tie and looked past me through the dusty window out over rooftops to a dull, leaden sky. He shook his head.

'Terrible,' he said.

We did agenting things like writing and accepting cheques, and I undertook to follow Miss Cummings around for a while and check on her friends and see if I could find out what was on her mind and stopping her from writing another blockbuster.

Thackeray had given me Cummings's schedule for the next couple of days and I planned to pick her up that night after a book launching in a city bookshop. The first thing I did after depositing the agent's cheque was go to my favourite bookshop in Glebe Point Road for a copy of *The Crying Gulls*. I usually buy my second-hand Penguins and remaindered sports books there, so the proprietor gave me an odd look when I handed over six bucks for something that felt like a house brick.

'You'll hate it,' he said. 'It's slop.'

'I'll use it to work on my pecs then.' I needed both hands to carry the book and I waved aside the five cents changed he offered. 'Give it to a poet,' I said.

The book's cover featured a sunburnt country scene with three figures standing on something reminiscent of Ayers Rock. The figure in the middle was a woman who looked like Olivia Newton-John dressed to boogy; the man on the left was a stockman who looked a bit like Clint Eastwood as Rowdy Yates; the man on the right resembled Steve McQueen in *The Thomas Crown Affair*. A banner read: 'Their love was thunder, their hatred was fire'. Great cover. I tossed the book into the Falcon and drove home for a drink.

Six hours later I watched from my car the unedifying sight of the bookshop disgorging the launchers. Some of them were pretty well launched themselves. I recognised a batch of well-known writers and a heroin addict artist. There were a couple of journalists I'd drunk with on odd occasions—men and women with a keen eye for the free glass.

A woman answering Thackeray's description of Carla Cummings was one of the last to leave. She was small, nothing over five feet in her high heeled shoes and she wore a tight, short black dress and a big red wig. She staggered a little and hailed a cab. Two men staggered with her. Cummings's glittery dress and wig and the white overcoat one of the men had thrown over his shoulders made them look stagey and unreal, like figures in a rock film clip.

If there's any work more boring that watching other people having a good time, I don't know of it.

Carla Cummings and her two mates had some people's definition of a *very* good time. I followed the taxi to the Cross where it dropped the threesome at a nightclub cum restaurant that boasts a fifties atmosphere. I parked illegally and when I got back Cummings was tucking into a huge dish of pasta. She ate sloppily and dropped her fork; she kept talking and her youngish companions, both well built, one dark one fair, kept laughing. That was the most fun she had. After drinking most of a bottle of red wine she went upstairs and danced with the men in turn. For someone as drunk as she was she danced pretty well, but I saw the strain on the dark guy's face as he half-held her up. After that they walked—her very unsteadily—along the street eyeing the whores. No one got many giggles out of that so they took a cab to a high-priced apartment block in Potts Point. I sat in my car and listened to the movement of the water as lights went on and off three floors up. The water kept moving but the windows stayed dark and I drove home.

I was back in Pott's Point at 8 a.m. and after an hour's wait I was rewarded by the arrival of a silver Honda Accord, driven by a sleek character with a cravat, a yachtsman's blazer and the trousers and tan to go with it. They drove to a breakfast place in the Cross where you can sit among the bricks and trees and watch the previous night's crap being swept up and carried away by the lower classes.

The yachtsman looked to be doing some serious talking in the car so I got a table within earshot of the pair and ordered coffee. In surveillance you can work this close just once.

Cummings ordered an iced coffee and the yachtsman had a straight black, like me. When the orders arrived the writer proceded to demolish a pale brown structure that looked like a model of Mont Blanc. She also had a plateful of croissants on the side. Her hand was shaking and she dropped some of the mixture on her dress where it joined last night's food and drink stains.

'I've been thinking it over, Leslie,' she said.

Les sipped coffee and didn't speak.

'He's irritating and moralistic, but he did a wonderful job for the first book.'

'It sold itself, dear. The thing is—can he do the same again?'

She filled her mouth with pastry and cold liquid; I had to look away, and I had the feeling that Leslie wanted to but he didn't.

'I don't know but that's not really what I'm worried about just now.'

He leaned forward solicitously. 'What *are* you worried about Carla? Can I help?'

She shook her head and crumbs sprayed on the table. 'I can't tell you, Leslie, but it is important to everything I do at the moment. It's driving me mad ...'

'You haven't signed a contract with Thackeray, have you?'

'No, of course not. Don't hound me, Leslie. It *is* about Joseph and when I get more reports ... when it's *settled* I'll let you know about your offer.'

He smiled, showed beautifully capped teeth, a sagging jawline and an over-used charm that was losing its candle power. There was an air of desperation about him which he was desperately anxious not to show—and it showed. He tilted a thin, brown hand that carried a wide gold ring.

'Just tell me, are you fifty/fifty in favour or ...'

She drained her drink with a soft slurp and blotted up some croissant crumbs with a bony finger. 'Sixty/forty,' she said. 'Can you run me home? I've got to change to give some ghastly talk.'

They got up, Cummings paid the bill the way she'd done the previous night, and they went streetwards. I let them go and ordered another coffee as an aid to thinking. There was some to do. Thackeray had more problems than he thought: I didn't like the sound of reports and a settlement. It smelled too much of what I did myself, and that threw up some interesting possibilities.

Thackeray's notes told me that Cummings was addressing the Hunters Hill Women's Literary Group later that morning. It sounded as missable as my own hanging, so I decided to widen my terms of reference a little and see what Mr Joseph Thackeray was doing.

Thackeray's office was in William Street, just a short walk from mine, but I didn't have to get to his door for things to become interesting. There was a bank across the road from the building Thackeray was in, and as I passed it I saw Rusty Fenton looking out through the smoked glass windows. Now a bank is one of the last places you'd expect to see Rusty. When he has money he gives it to barmen not tellers. Rusty didn't see me so I went into the bank by a side door and watched him. I've never known Rusty not to work in close harness with 'Bomber' Stafford and, sure enough, after a minute or so Stafford came hurrying out of Thackeray's building and across the street. Rusty shot out to meet him, they had a quick confab and ran back across the street, defying the traffic. I watched through the smoked glass: Rusty and Stafford got into a van; Joseph Thackeray came out onto the street and looked up and down expectantly. He had on another silly, spotted bow tie; he still looked narrow and wispy and the smoked glass gave his skin an unhealthy grey sheen. A taxi pulled up,

Thackeray got in and Rusty and Stafford followed it on up the hill towards the Cross.

Out of habit I jotted the numbers of the taxi and the van on the back of a withdrawal slip. I could find out where Thackeray had gone easily enough, but I was more interested in why Rusty and 'Bomber' were interested in him. Rusty has a lot of trades—police informer, leg man for a few people in my game, small time fence. 'Bomber' Stafford quit the ring after an undistinguished career as a prelim boy and prelim old man. He'd done some standing-over since then and worked for security services and some corner-cutting private enquiry men. He'd do just about anything that didn't require any brains, he knew his limitations. Working with Rusty topped up their collective IQ, but not by all that much.

A phone call to Thackeray's office brought me the information that he was attending the opening of a photography exhibition in Paddington. I drove there and parked down the street. Rusty and 'Bomber' were sitting in their van drinking beer and watching the place. Rusty put down his beer can and wrote something in a notebook. I shuddered to think of his spelling but I'd have liked to get a look at the notebook. I could have fronted them but even Rusty knows enough to keep his mouth shut when he's working and 'Bomber' might just get lucky with a punch. Things were coming together in my mind: Cummings mentioned reports on Thackeray and here was Rusty Fenton on surveillance, sucking his pencil and making notes. Rusty could report to someone else who could make some sense of what he said and report in turn to Cummings. Who?

It was becoming ridiculous; the only course I could think of was to follow Rusty—I felt I was getting a long way from my brief but hell, anything was better than the Hunters Hill affair. The photography exhibition must have included eats because Thackeray stayed a few hours, and was wiping his mouth with a spotted handkerchief when he left. Rusty had sent 'Bomber' for pies; I had no one to send so I missed lunch. Thackeray walked off the canapes with a stroll through some of the pricier streets of Paddo to a tall, well-appointed terrace in the priciest street of them all. Rusty's van crawled along after him and I crawled along too. It was a wonder the Shark Patrol didn't spot us and report us for suspicious conduct. It was mid-afternoon and pretty warm; Rusty and 'Bomber' seemed happy to park outside the house but then, Rusty could send 'Bomber' for beer. I wasn't prepared to wait.

After Paddington, the back streets of the Cross felt like Bangkok. I parked the Falcon on the concrete patch Primo Tomasetti, the best tattooist in the country, rents to me and went to see the artist himself. My recollection was that 'Bomber' had been a client of Primo's not so long back.

'Hi, Cliff.' Primo was bent over a hairy forearm, trying to shave it without drawing blood. The young man being operated on was gritting his teeth and looking away. He didn't seem to be quite the type for what he was doing. Primo wiped the suds off.

'Go have a look at the designs my son,' he said. 'I gotta talk white slavery with my friend here.'

The tattooee-to-be walked shakily across to a wall poster covered with signs erotic, nautical and extra terrestrial.

'You sure he can take it?' I whispered.

'We'll see. Some people, it turns them on. Gets messy here sometimes. Did you know that? Do you care?'

'I learn something new from you every time we meet, Primo. Remember when you did a little job on 'Bomber' Stafford?'

'Sure. Last month.'

'He have much to say?'

'"Bomber"? Talking's not his thing. Just said he needed the tattoo for his come back.'

'His what?'

'His come back, in the ring. He reckoned tattoos were all the go—all the fighters got 'em. I told him to forget the come back; stick to stealing I said.'

'What'd he say?'

The gilded youth was stroking his smooth forearm and looking impatient. Primo caught the look and moved away from me. 'He reckoned he was serious and that Rusty was helping him, training with him. Gotta work, Cliff.'

'Thanks, Primo. Training where and when?'

'Trueman's he said, most nights. He was serious about getting himself punchy.'

Trueman's gym is not a place a fighter goes to when he's on the way up. It sits in a back street in Newtown behind a faded sign that hasn't been really bright since Vic Patrick retired. It was after seven when I got there, getting dark and cool. Rusty's van was parked outside Trueman's. The street smelled of old air and the air in Sammy's gym smelled of old bodies and old hopes and dreams.

I stood on the dusty boards and looked at the sweat-stained ring and the cracked leather of the heavy bag and speed ball. The only new things in the place were the cigarette butts in the smokers' bins. 'Bomber' Stafford was lumbering through a skipping routine in one corner of the gym and Rusty was working on an exercise bicycle. A thin Aborigine wandered over to the speed ball and began setting up a pretty good rhythm on it. He was better to watch than 'Bomber' but I was disappointed to see so few people in the place. My chances of getting a sneaky look through

Rusty's locker looked slim.

'Hey, Cliff; Cliff Hardy!' 'Bomber' concentrated hard to skip and talk at the same time.

' "Bomber".'

'Come to work out?'

I had a bag of bits and pieces in my hand, more for show than anything but as I looked 'Bomber's' flabby torso over I had an idea.

'Yeah. You want to go a round or two?'

Out of the corner of my eye I could see Rusty shaking his head but 'Bomber' ignored him. He dropped the rope, went over to an equipment locker and pulled out two pairs of battered gloves. He tossed one set to me.

'Let's have a go.'

I caught the gloves and went back to the locker room at the end of the gym. It smelt of sweat and was poorly lit; only two of the lockers were closed. There were a few clothes and magazines sticking out of others but Rusty and 'Bomber' were security conscious. I reckoned the locks would take me about thirty seconds apiece. I stripped, put on running shoes, shorts and singlet and went out pulling on the gloves. 'Bomber' was in the ring already, and Rusty was in his corner bending his ear. The Aborigine and another pug who'd appeared from somewhere were standing expectantly by the ropes. I slipped under and jogged a bit to get the feel of the canvas.

'This is bloody crazy,' Rusty said. ' "Bomber" outweighs you by a stone, Hardy. There's no bloody resin, the ropes're slack . . .'

'Just a spar, isn't it "Bomber"? Three rounds do you? One of you blokes keep time?'

The Aborigine glanced up at the wall clock and grinned.

'Time,' he said harshly.

I'd never fought professionally and was only average as an amateur, but I knew what to do against an overweight slob like 'Bomber' Stafford. You handle a guy like that in one of two ways, or both ways if you can do it: you wear him down or you get him off balance. I didn't have time to wear him down. 'Bomber' came out swinging, and I ducked and weaved and let him miss. I went in and under a couple of times and dug hard punches into his gut. I left his head alone, heads are easy to miss. At the end of three minutes he was blowing hard and Rusty was muttering about stopping it. But 'Bomber' came out for more; this time I baulked and changed pace on him and worked him first this way, then that. He landed one punch—a looping left that I saw a bit late. It hurt but Stafford was off balance with surprise when it landed. I moved up, feinted, moved the wrong way and hit him with a left hook as good as any I'd ever thrown. Then I hit him on the point with an unorthodox short right; his eyes rolled back and he hit the deck.

I was out of the ring and heading for the lockers almost before he landed. I heard Rusty cursing and calling for water. I was breathing hard but I pulled the gloves off and got my fingers working in overdrive. The first locker I teased open was obviously 'Bomber's' and I flipped it shut. Rusty's jacket was hanging in the other locker and I had the notebook out of the breast pocket and open with the pages flicking over in record time. Rusty's notes were semi-literate, like: 'We seen Thacaray go ina sort of picture show place and we wait car'. Folded into the book was a carbon copy sheet, neatly typed, which elaborated on Rusty's scrawl and looked like a professional surveillance report. Items like 'Subject entered restaurant at 20.00 hours and met three individuals male and one female (see below for descriptions)'. The bits I read amounted to nothing, but looked good, being only loosely based on Rusty's data—a lot of poetic licence in it. The only indication of who the poet might be was a phone number carefully printed on the pages before Rusty's notes began. I committed it to memory and put the book back and closed the locker.

'No shower, Cliff boy?' Fat Sammy Trueman waddled into the locker room as I was pulling my shirt on. His shirt ballooned out in front of him and his chins almost met the swell. Sammy had been a good lightweight a long time ago. I kept dressing.

'In a rush.'

'Great bit of work, didn't know you could handle yourself ...' He broke off to wheeze and cough—the sorts of terminal sounds he's been making for twenty years. '... like that.'

'He was a sitting duck. Hope you're not encouraging this comeback bullshit.'

Trueman shrugged the shrug he'd given over a hundred prelim boys and a dozen punchdrunk main eventers. It was a ten per cent of something is something shrug. I stuffed my togs in my bag, pushed past him and went out of the gym fast.

As soon as I got to the car I scribbled down the telephone number hoping it wasn't just the number for Rusty's bookie. At home, I poured a big glass of wine and sat down by the phone. The recorded message was in a voice I knew better than I cared to: 'You have called Holland Investigations. Thank you for calling. The office is unattended but if you leave your name and number Mr Holland or one of his associates will contact you in business hours. Speak after the beep please.'

I put Cleo Laine on the stereo and thought about it. Reg 'Woolfie' Holland was one of the shonkiest operators in my shonky trade. He'd had a couple of convictions way back, but had kept his nose clean long enough to get a licence. I had *never* heard anything complimentary about his competence or honesty, and there're not many people you can say that about. He'd used Rusty and Stafford as leg men before I knew, and now I could smell one of the oldest scams in the book—they'd probably been doing it in Pompeii.

It was getting late and the four or five minutes dancing with 'Bomber', plus the tension had tired me; on the other hand the wine had relaxed me. A hundred and twenty-five bucks gets you a twenty-four-hour-day if need be. I finished the wine, resisted another glass, and went upstairs to get my burglar's suit on.

'Woolfie's' office was a hole-in-the-wall in Surry Hills, as far as you can get from the fashionable coffee bars and still be in the locality. I remembered a heated discussion I'd had there with 'Woolfie' a few years back when he'd attempted to barge in on a case of mine. Blows hadn't quite been struck but voices had been raised. Out of habit I'd noticed 'Woolfie's' set-up and hadn't been impressed. It had looked like an easy nut to crack, and it was; there was a lane at the back, a brick fence and a window that was child's play. 'Woolfie' shared the space with Terry Collins, Hair Restoration and Scalp Revitalisation—Satisfaction Guaranteed and Chloe Smith, Literary Agent.

The office was a two-room affair both smelling of 'Woolfie's' sixty-a-day cigarette habit. The answering machine was the only concession to style. The filing cabinets were an insult to a man who can open boxing gym lockers and back windows. I was thumbing through the files within seconds while holding a pencil torch in my teeth. Holland's files were a mess, but like all of us self-employed types he had to keep some sort of record so that the taxation office wouldn't immure him. The Carla Cummings file was a model of its kind. It opened with notes on a meeting between Cummings and 'Woolfie' and his engagement to investigate an accusation against Joseph Thackeray which was made in an anonymous letter to the author. A photocopy of the letter was enclosed, several copies in fact. The letter was undated, but the first Cummings-Holland meeting was six weeks back. Carbon copies of 'Woolfie's' reports were enclosed; they were all like the sheet I'd seen in Rusty's notebook. One thing was sure, 'Woolfie' hadn't written them unless he'd been going to night classes since I'd last seen him. I'd have bet anything though that he *had* written the original anonymous letter to set up the classic blackmail situation—get yourself hired and charge top dollar to investigate a threat that comes from yourself. Depending on how you play it you can spin it out as long as you like and, with a bit of finesse, wind it up so that everybody's happy. 'Woolfie' had milked it for three thousand already. It's an oldie but goodie; some people in the game used to regard it as almost legal.

I checked by pecking a character or two on the office Olivetti, but even 'Woolfie' wasn't dumb enough to type the letter in the office. It was done on an upright electric, not the sort of thing he'd be likely to have at home. Proof, that's the problem with exposing this sort of deal. I took one of the photocopies, leaving three, and went out the way I'd come. I went down the lane the other way and walked along the street onto which Holland's office fronted to where I'd left the Falcon outside an instant printing shop.

I slept on it and sat down with coffee and strong light the next morning to look at the letter:

DEAR CARLA CUMMINGS
Your agent Mr Thackeray is a crook. He is robbing you blind. Have you made a will? He is conspiring with other parties to rob you even after you are dead. And that may not be long.

A friend.

Some friend. I stared at the lines on the photocopy paper until they blurred. I made coffee and drank it and poured wine and drank that too. *The Singing Gulls* was sitting, unopened, on the table and I looked idly at the beginning:

Kelly's hopes soared as the cloud of dust on the horizon took firmer shape. She knew it would be Mark and that soon she would feel him holding her and her white silk dress would be grimy from his dust and sweat and that she wouldn't care . . .

I almost gagged and slammed the book down on top of the note. Its straight edge defined something I hadn't seen before—the original letter had been trimmed by a paper guillotine, possibly to remove a watermark. The guillotine blade must have had a nick out of it or a wobble because there was an irregularity in the trimmed edge. 'Woolfie's' photocopy was A4 size, but had originally been on a sheet twice that size which had been halved by a guillotine stroke. Same nick or wobble.

I sat back and drank some more wine. Dumb 'Woolfie'. Two pairs of scissors and he'd have had no problems. That set me thinking about paper guillotines and that train of thought led directly to the instant printing place across the road from Holland's office. Dumb, but that dumb?

One blade stroke through a sheet of quarto in the print shop showed me that 'Woolfie' had fouled up.

No point in wasting time. I went across the street and went up to the office of Reginald Holland, Private Enquiries, to make my private accusations. 'Woolfie' was in his shirt sleeves, which were dirty as the whole surface of him and many surfaces round about are dirty from his cigarette ash. His face was prune-like from trying to function through the fug and his dark hair was thin and defeated-looking. But 'Woolfie' is big and bulky, and he uses the bulk to intimidate when he can. I hadn't knocked and he looked annoyed.

'Piss off, Hardy.'

'Don't be like that 'Woolfie', we've got things to talk about.'

'Yeah, like why you belted up the "Bomber".'

'The "Bomber's" not even a Tiger Moth anymore, you know that.'

'I'm busy, Hardy, I don't need your crummy jokes this time of the day, or anytime.'

'Busy at what?'

He glared at me and lit another cigarette from the stub of the last. His teeth were as brown as his fingers and the air was like in a billiard room at midnight. I didn't want to spend anymore time with him than I had to. I took the sheets of paper out and smoothed them on his desk top.

'Oldest one around, Holland, someone used it on Mae West when she was a girl. How'd you get yourself fixed up to do the investigation?'

What passed across his face almost made me feel sorry for him; it was a *'Oh no, caught again!'* look combined with a flicker of hope that I didn't have the proof and maybe a bit of bluster coming up.

'You used the paper cutter across the road on the note and the copies, sport—that puts you right in it.' I blew on my palm. 'There goes your licence. What's a three thousand dollar fraud worth these days? Couple of years?'

He put down his cigarette, dropped the hand to a drawer, slid it open and pointed a dusty-looking .38 at me. I laughed.

'Don't be silly 'Woolfie'. I don't want you. I'll take the money out of your hide if I have to, but I don't want you.'

The gun wavered and he put it down and picked up the cigarette again—easier to kill yourself than someone else.

'What d'you want?' he croaked.

'Whoever put you up to it. Whoever wrote the reports and stands to gain. Straight deal—you tell me and I don't tell anyone how naughty you've been.'

He groaned. 'She'll kill me.'

We went across the hall to Chloe Smith's office, and as soon as 'Woolfie' came in, with me manful and commanding by his shoulder, she knew that her latest dream was a fizzer. She was a redhead, redder now than she had been once, and the dye job had hardened her features. Her thin face was beaky and aggrieved despite the touched up brightness of her eyes and lips. She looked at 'Woolfie' as if she was seeing him as he was for the first time.

'He knows,' she said.

'Woolfie' nodded and dropped into a chair in front of her desk. He dislodged a pile of manuscripts which cascaded over the floor in their loose-leaf binders, manilla folders and exercise books. There were a lot of manuscripts in the room and the shelf that carried the line 'Client's works' had only a few, thin volumes on it.

As it came out it was a typical loser's story. Smith and Holland had convinced each other that they could pull off the big one—that 'Woolfie' could milk Carla Cummings for enough money to enable Chloe to put on a good enough front to get Cummings to come over to her once 'Woolfie' had sown enough seeds of doubt about Thackeray. She showed me the letterheads she'd had planned and told me about the flash office she was going to rent in Paddington. Smith had got wind that Cummings's next book was to be a private eye yarn and 'Woolfie' had turned up at the right time—just after the letter about Thackeray had been delivered—to offer himself as an informant initially and then as an investigator.

'It wouldn't have worked,' I said. 'She has this yachting type with capped teeth sniffing at her for his ten per cent, probably others as well.'

Chloe flared at that. 'It *would* have worked! Reginald would have influenced her to accept my services.'

'Reginald Who?' I said. 'Woolfie' lit another cigarette.

'What are you going to do, Hardy?' he asked.

'How much of the money can you give back?'

He shrugged. 'Half.'

'I'll take that and talk to Thackeray and Cummings. She might think she got her money's worth in a funny way. You never know, 'Woolfie', you might end up in her next book.'

I smiled, but they didn't. I got a cheque from 'Woolfie' and got out of his office before my clothes smelled as bad as his. For no good reason I'd brought *The Singing Gulls* with me from home, and I grabbed it out of the car and went back to Holland's office. He looked at me through the haze with red, tormented eyes.

'What now, Hardy?'

I threw the book on his desk. 'Read that,' I said. 'Part of your punishment.'

Rhythm Track

He was wearing the oldest T-shirt I'd ever seen; it was a faded blue, tattered around the neck and sleeve ends, and had holes everywhere. The almost obliterated letters across the chest read CREDENCE. His thin, nicotine-stained fingers flew across a couple of thousand buttons and switches, then he sighed and poured himself a cap full of Jack Daniels Tennessee whisky. He tossed the drink off, capped the bottle and picked up an electric guitar.

'What's he doing?' I whispered.

'Rhythm track,' Vance Hill said. 'Shh.'

I shushed and watched the strong fingers dance along the frets as he strummed; his long black hair flopped as he jerked his head convulsively. After a few seconds he nodded, flipped a switch and the studio filled with the music. He strummed and jerked for a few seconds and the jumpy chords he was hitting seemed to sit in the air in front of him. I wanted to tap my foot but kept it still. After a few seconds he said 'Shit!' and hit a button. The music stopped.

He took another drink and lit a menthol cigarette. When he turned around to face Hill he looked about five times older than his fifteen-year-old T-shirt.

'You hear it? Nowhere near blappy enough. I can't get it. I try for more blappy and I just get blah-balah. We need Tim.'

'Easy, Con, we'll get him. This is Cliff Hardy, he's a private investigator—finds people. Right, Hardy?'

'Sometimes,' I said. I nodded to Con, who acknowledged me with a double puff on his cigarette. 'You seemed to be doing all right to me.'

He shook his head. 'I was doing lousy. I'm a keyboards man. Without a good rhythm track this'll sound like shit.'

'I just brought you in here to give you the feel, Hardy.' Hill said. 'Let's go outside and talk. Don't worry, Con.'

'I won't breathe either,' Con said. He pushed some more buttons and we went out of the studio.

The place was packed into a high, narrow-fronted building in Annandale. Outside the studio door there was a narrow passage leading to a narrow office and reception area. Hill waved me into a chair and lifted his hand to a young woman who was answering a telephone behind the glass panel. She grimaced and made a throttling motion with one hand.

'Want some coffee, Hardy? Drink or anything?'

'No, thanks.' I got out my notebook and balanced it on my knee. The denim under it was fashionably faded but unfashionably thin and non-stretch. 'Tim Talbot's his name. That real, or nom de stage?'

'Real. Tim's a studio muso, I doubt if he's ever been on a stage.'

'Introvert?'

Vance Hill looked as if he'd heard the word before but couldn't quite remember what it meant. The young woman came to his aid. She'd slipped out from behind the glass and into a chair near mine.

'Yes,' she said. 'He is.'

'Hardy, this is Ro Bush. Ro, Cliff Hardy.'

We nodded at each other. She was a brunette with very white teeth, lustrous brown eyes and an athletic figure. I was nodding in approval as well as greeting. She wore a white sleeveless top and jeans,

149

no jewellery, short fingernails and an intelligent expression.

'Tim's shy,' she said, 'withdrawn even. He doesn't get on with many people. He's also tremendously talented.' She shot a look at the door that led to the studio which I interpreted as saying that not everyone on the premises was equally talented.

Hill leaned forward in his chair. 'Like I said on the phone, we're working on the theme song for *The Dying Game*. Great song, sure hit. Tim wrote it and started on the recording with Con and a couple of others. The vocal's fine and we can probably do something with the bass track, but there's some mandolin to go on and a rhythm track needed. Tim's the only guy who can do it. Jesus, just the rough demo he laid down sounds a hundred times better than anything else we've tried.'

'When's the last time you saw him?'

Hill looked at the woman. 'Week ago?'

She nodded. 'Week and a day.'

'Why'd he leave?'

'He had a fight with Sport and Con,' Ro Bush sighed. 'And me and Vance for that matter.'

'What sort of fight?'

'Artistic,' she said. 'Tim didn't want strings and choir, he wanted a smaller, rougher sound.'

'Won't do,' Hill snapped. He was about my age or a bit younger but his energy seemed to have run out. He wasn't fat, but tired and slumped he looked it. His skin was greyish and his eyes had an unhealthy, fishy look. 'This is for a movie, a *big* movie; it opens with wide shots, we've gotta have the treatment on the song.'

Ro Bush shrugged the way you do when you've heard something twenty times before. 'Tim argues the opposite—big visuals, small sound.'

I grinned at her. 'Who's right?'

'Tim,' she said.

Hill groaned. 'The money's right, like always, and the money says give it the treatment. Christ!'

'That's it,' she said. 'Back and forth for a few hours, then Tim storms off—this is around dawn you understand—and that's the last anyone's seen of him.'

I scribbled. 'This is Tuesday, a.m.? Right?'

Hill nodded.

'How much booze?'

'In who?'

'In everyone.'

'Lots,' Ro Bush said. 'There always is, they were all drunk except me. I get sick if I drink very much.'

'Drugs?'

Hill shrugged. 'Sometimes, not that night I don't think.'

'Talbot uses drugs?'

'They all do,' she said. 'Tim's no different.'

'Terrific. Okay, well I'll need the names and addresses of all the disputants, picture of Talbot, some ideas about his friends, how he spends his time and so on. Who can give me that?'

'I can.' She got up and went behind the glass. I thought there was something shifty about the look Hill was giving me and there was no point in just noting the fact in my notebook.

'This doesn't quite hang together, Mr Hill. The police could look for him, or his Mum or someone. What do you know that I don't know?'

Hill made a face like a man having wind trouble. 'You said it before—Talbot's heavily into drugs. He's supposed to be clean at the moment but this could've set him off. If the cops find him they could have something on him—he's no good to me in Long Bay.'

I grunted. 'Exactly who is who around here?'

'I'm the boss of the record company, independent outfit—Centre Records. I'm the executive producer on this movie theme. Ro's the manager of the studio here, smart girl.'

I'd been around long enough to ask the right question. '*Executive* producer, who's the actual producer?'

Hill looked even more uncomfortable. 'Not settled,' he said. He handed me a card and a plain door key. 'Can I assume you'll do it?'

'I'll take a look, sure. A hundred and twenty-five a day and expenses.'

'My number's on the card. That's a key to Tim's place.' He took a deep breath and tried to straighten his shoulders. He went back towards the studio and the shoulders had slumped again after the first step.

'Here you are, Mr Hardy.' Ro Bush handed me a typed sheet and a magazine clipping. The photo showed three men lounging against a big convertible which was full of musical instruments. The car had STEAM CLEANING stencilled on the side. One of the short fingernails touched the faces. 'That's Sport Gordon, that's Jerry Leakey, don't know what happened to him. Here's Tim.'

Talbot looked ill at ease in the company of the others; he was hanging on to the neck of a guitar sticking out of the car like a boy holding his mother's hand. He was thin and young with a lot of hair; the thinnest part of him was his nose which was long and looked to be scarcely wider than my little finger. A crease ran across Jerry's face which was perhaps symptomatic, but Sport Gordon presented full face and full force. He was muscular in a singlet and tight jeans, looking like young building workers do before the beer gets to them.

'Steam Cleaning were pretty big a year or so ago. Sport did the vocal for the theme song by the way.'

Ro Bush smelled of something good and as she didn't come much above my shoulder it was easy to sniff without being impolite.

'Hill said that Talbot wasn't a performer.'

'He's not, not really. Steam Cleaning were more of a studio band. They did some gigs, a few big ones too, but Tim played with his back to the audience most of the time.'

'I've never heard of them,' I said. 'But that doesn't mean much, the last live band I saw was the Rolling Stones.'

It wasn't the way to her heart. 'We call them the M'n M's around here.'

'What's that mean?'

'You know—the little sweets, like smarties.'

I shook my head.

'Also the multi-millionaires. See?'

'I suppose so. What happened to ... Steam Cleaning?'

She shrugged. 'They broke up. Nothing unusual—problems between Sport and Tim. They were the writers.'

I couldn't resist it. 'Like Lennon and McCartney? Jagger and Richard?'

'Mm, I don't think they'd be flattered by the comparison.'

'How come Sport's singing now, then?'

'Oh, that's not strange. Tim's the writer and the producer, and he picks the vocalist. Sport's got a great voice.'

I stored away the difference between Hill and Bush on the producer question and looked at the sheet. There were half a dozen names and addresses including Sport Gordon and Ro Bush. She studied me as I studied the list.

'I consider myself a friend,' she said.

'We all need them. Thanks Miss Bush.'

'Ro.'

'Okay.' I tapped the paper. 'Music and cars?'

She nodded. 'Tim builds them, modifies them, drives like he plays—excellently.'

'How much looking has anyone done?'

'Not much. Vance called in at his flat. Nothing there. I rang Sport and Ian—they're on the list. They hadn't seen him. His family's interstate, Brisbane I think.'

'You're the only woman on the list.' I looked at her enquiringly.

She shook her head. 'No to what you're thinking. He's shy.'

'I really need to know the economics and politics of this. This record's important to who?'

'Everyone: Vance needs a hit to get his label moving; Tim and the other session musos all need the money; Sport's doing all right solo but he could use a hit single; the movie needs its theme.'

'What about you?'

'We get paid for the studio time. Doesn't hurt to have nurtured a hit but there's nothing riding on it for me, really. I'm worried about Tim, though.'

'You sound like the only one who is. Hill's worried about his hit and Con's worried about his blaps.' I looked at the paper again. 'Con's not on it.'

'Con's a creep and he's out of his depth. I'm sorry, I have to get back to work. There's more than one bloody record being made here although you wouldn't know it sometimes.'

I took a card from her too and went out onto the street. It was 11 p.m. an unusual time to start on an investigation but Hill had told me when he'd phoned in the afternoon that the musicians didn't start work until night fell and kept at it until dawn. He'd wanted me to get the feel and I suppose I had: booze, drugs, temperamental outbursts and blaps all being recorded on thirty-two tracks. I couldn't help thinking of post-1970 pop music as a sick combination of adolescence and money; I didn't feel comfortable with the matter but then, I'd once found a missing Jamaican marriage celebrant who'd specialised in Rastafarian weddings and I hadn't felt comfortable with him either.

Talbot's address was in Glebe, handy to home. I drove down towards the water and took the last turn to the right. The street was dog-legged, with big buildings on either side. Talbot's flat turned out to be a bed-sitter in the back of a house that had no water view. I picked my way down the dark corridors where one light in three worked. The key turned easily in the lock and I stepped into a room of stale smells.

I have a friend who claims he can tell how much time has elapsed since anyone farted in a room. He says it's never very long in a lived-in place. I'd have bet on a week here. The room had a bed, some books, three guitars in cases, a saucer with a few roaches in it and a pair of jeans, three T-shirts and a zip jacket. The guitar cases were the only items that got a regular dusting. The kitchenette had a half-loaf of green bread and a lump of ant-covered butter on a laminex table and a few basic bits of cutlery. There was milk in the fridge and some cans of Country Special beer.

I opened one of the cans, sat on the bed and drank it. No letters from Brisbane, no suicide note, no ripped mattress, no blood. The room was neither cheerful nor depressing; there'd be some natural light in the daytime and it seemed quiet now. The carpet didn't stick to the feet and nothing big scuttled in the corners. I finished the beer and belched—that'd have to do for occupancy. I let myself out and drove home.

The next two days' work was just as unprofitable. I

tramped around the addresses Ro had given me and used the phone like Billy McMahon. In a city restaurant I talked briefly to Sport Gordon, whose chief amusements seemed to be flexing his muscles and shaking his head. I listened to impossible jargon in shops that specialised in gear for customising cars.

Talbot's own car was said to be a silvered Mazda with many refinements which he kept in a parking bay at a big block of flats near his rooming house by arrangement with a non car-owning resident. I located the resident and was shown the empty parking space. As with the room, the rent for the space was paid up until the end of the month. I reported the car stolen, giving my name and phone number, and expected a call on it about as much as you expect the good news from the lottery office.

I went back to Talbot's room, drank some more of his beer, and found some papers in a guitar case. He had a couple of hundred dollars in a savings account and a bit more in a cheque account. He had ninety dollars in USA currency which was increasing in value just sitting there in the dark—or so they tell me. Telephone numbers were scrawled on the back of a sheet of music, and I rang them, drawing blanks every time. A guitar shop, more mag wheels, a dentist and his mother in Brisbane, I pretended to be a record producer and asked for news of Tim.

'Timothy?' the stiff voice came back. 'I'm afraid we're not in touch. How did you get this number?'

I ducked that and left my number in case she heard. I guessed she didn't even bother to write it down. After putting it off for as long as possible, I rang Hill with the bad news.

'Shit,' he said. 'An impasse?' He pronounced it with a hard 'a' like the American he was working hard at pretending to be.

'Looks like it. I've got a few connections to the

junkie scene, but I got blank walls there too. What's happening with the record?'

'I'm stalling the producers is what's happening. Con's going out of his mind.'

I realised that Con was the only card in the pack I hadn't paid attention to and I knew why. I'd accepted Ro's assessment of him—not very professional. I told Hill there were still a few leads to follow and rang off. A call to the studio got Ro who told me that Con would be in around eight; she made him sound about as welcome as AIDS.

'What d'you want him for?'

'Just a talk. Would you have time for a drink a bit before then?'

She said she would and I was there at seven. At a quarter past we were in the bar of the North Annandale trying to hear ourselves talk above the country'n western band.

'How's their sound?' I yelled.

'Lousy,' she shouted, 'but who's listening?'

She was wearing a black top and white jeans this time and looked just as good. I grilled her about the music business, because my feeling was that it was at the heart of the matter. Something about the look on Con's face when he couldn't get blappy, something about Talbot's carefully maintained guitars and about Ro Bush's intelligent, careful assessments of the musicians' talents and potential made me feel as if I was in the presence of a sort of religious fervour. Hardy's law is that religion screws people up as much as other things, maybe more.

Ro Bush was a business-like lady and it didn't seem inappropriate to take a look at my notebook while we were talking. I ordered a second drink and she unloosened a bit.

'Will this go on Vance's bill?'

'Sure.'

'Good.' She smiled and took a solid sip.

'Is *The Dying Game* really that good?'

'I dunno. Haven't seen it. I doubt it, some old hack wrote the script.'

'I meant the song.'

'Oh, the song. It's not called *The Dying Game*, it's ... *Bloody Nose Blues* or something.'

'Doesn't it have to have the film title in the lyrics somewhere?'

'Evidently not; it doesn't, I know that.'

'Mm, when do they copyright a song?'

'Depends, sometimes when the record contract's signed, that's if the song's already written; sometimes when the record's due for release.' She finished her drink and smiled again. 'Better get back—thanks, Vance.'

Con was in the studio wearing the same T-shirt and looking even more harassed. My arrival didn't help.

'Shit,' he said. 'I was hoping to do some work.' He drank a cap of Old Grandad to prove his point.

'You can work. Just tell me about the fight that went on before Tim Talbot left.'

'I can do better than that. Had a mike open.' He flipped and pushed things on the console and a voice filled the room:

'Fuck you!' the voice said. 'I wrote the fuckin' thing.'

'You think you're bloody God, Tim. I changed the fuckin' lyrics as I sang it, you didn't even fuckin' notice and now you want the credit.'

'I wrote every note, every word.'

'Wrote! What d'you fuckin' mean, wrote? Where is it?'

'In me fuckin' head.'

'What a crap heap that'd be—have another hit, Tim.'

'I'm straight, Sport.'

This was followed by some laughter, a few guitar chords and a strangled yell. Con cut the sound.

'What happened?' I said.

'Sport punched him. Tim split.'

'Who was in the right? I mean about the song?'

Con shrugged and a sharp bone stuck up out of a hole near the neckband of his T-shirt. 'Who knows? Tim wouldn't have written anything down at that stage. Sport's right there.'

'Play me the song and I'll leave you in peace.'

The bony fingers began their console minuet again. 'Rough mix,' he said, 'accent on rough.'

The studio filled with drums and guitars and a wailing chorus. All that stopped and a voice that sounded like it was coming from under a door croaked and muttered through some verses about blood and broken bones. The guitars cut in from time to time. The whole thing ended with a noise like a symphony orchestra falling into a snake pit.

'Jesus,' I said.

'Great isn't it? Or could be if we could get that rhythm track.'

'Didn't Talbot want it quieter.'

'Yeah.' He flipped and punched; I could see the big spools over in the corner of the studio spin and stop. The music was familar this time—the jumpy sound Con had been trying to match his guitar to on my first visit. I tapped my foot and Con looked at me before taking another cap of bourbon. I got up.

'I'm with Tim,' I said. 'I'm keener than ever to find him.'

Sport Gordon lived in Bellevue Hill, off Victoria Road. His house was well back behind a high wall with big iron gates that were standing half-open when I arrived. I parked further up the street and admired the water view in one direction and the glow from the city in the other. This was one rock star who'd apparently done all right. The house was a low, rambling affair, half-wrapped around a swimming pool and a pebbles-and-pot-plants garden. There was a lot of glass and polished wood, and a three vehicle carport.

There were lights on in the house but I couldn't see any movement, although some of the drapes were drawn back. I went through the gates and took a routine look at the carport. A white Mercedes sports car was sticking out, front first and slightly slewed, from one of the spaces and the car next to that was covered. I went over and lifted a corner of the tarpaulin: the sloping shapes of a Mazda RX7 gleamed silver under the moonlight.

That put a different slant on things. I went back to the car and got my S & W .38 ; I threaded the hip holster onto my belt and tucked the gun away at the back. I sneaked through the gates and went quickly to the side of the house and worked my way back in the shadows. I never heard of anyone who kept the door that led out to the pool properly connected to the alarm system and Gordon was no exception. I crouched down out of the light thrown up from the pool and tried to gauge the amount of movement in the house and where it was coming from. It didn't take long; there wasn't any sound and no movement either.

I stepped in and began a quiet prowl of the rooms. There was a lavishly stocked kitchen, a couple of opulent bathrooms and several bedrooms, big and small. One of the smaller ones was interesting—there were heavy webbing straps attached to the bed frame and slots for the ends of the straps to lock into. It looked newly installed, and a bit too practical for bondage fun'n games.

The signs were that three or four people were using the house but the place was as silent as the grave. I found the reason for that at the end of a passage on the side of the house away from the pool. The heavy padded door and glowing light above it meant recording studio.

Out by the pool again and round the back, bent low. I fetched up by the window into the studio and lifted an eye up to the bottom inch of the glass. Sport Gordon was there in his cut-off T-shirt along with another muscle man who was sitting at a console like the one in Annandale. Tim Talbot was hunched over a guitar, strumming hard and looking scared. He stopped; the console operator swore and flipped switches. Gordon took two steps and whacked Talbot across the face with a half-closed hand. Talbot's head jerked back on his thin neck.

I ducked down and scooted back into the house. Sound studio doors don't have catches, they just swing in, silently and smoothly. I took out the gun, pushed the door open and went in, side-stepping equipment and cables. Gordon recognised me and shouted something that was inaudible over the music. I told him to shut up and I gestured with the gun at the switch flipper. He cut the sound. Talbot had blood trickling down from his mouth and was the colour of old mortar.

'Get up,' I said. 'We're going.'

'Like fuck!' Gordon bullocked forward and I brought the gun up to level at the bridge of his nose. I didn't move back.

'Rock stars die young,' I said.

Talbot threw the guitar down, shot up out of his chair and rushed under the gun. He bolted through the door, yelling, tripping on cables but staying upright.

Sport Gordon threw a good punch that got me on

the shoulder and loosened my grip on the gun. But he didn't have the combination and while he was getting set for the next one I clipped him with a light left on the ear. He yelled and covered it with his hand; I chopped him across the throat and he covered that with his other hand. Maybe he was thinking of his precious vocal chords. The other man didn't move.

I ran out of the studio, jumping the cables, and skidded out onto the tiles beside the pool. I heard the car engine start, then the turning tyres screamed across the concrete and there was a bang as the sports car clipped the gate. It was heading up the hill as I reached the street. I belted along to my car and got it started and into a U-turn before I realised I still had the .38 in my hand. I threw it behind me and settled down to follow the Mercedes that was fifteen years younger, 50 kilometres an hour faster and driven by a madman.

Talbot took streets that would lead to the short freeway and the city. He took the turns fast and tight, and terrorised any cars that looked likely to check him. I followed as closely as I could which wasn't very, but I still managed to keep moving through the wake of stopped cars and irate drivers he left behind him.

He could drive all right, at least at first; at times all I had to keep in sight were his flashing brake lights. But something started to get to him and the Merc was weaving as it came off the freeway and roared down beside Centennial Park. I crowded up behind him after he hesitated at the Oxford Street turn. He dropped a gear and ripped past a taxi and through a red light.

He'd been shitting on the speed limit for more than ten minutes and still there were no flashing lights or sirens. It couldn't last. We were howling along through Paddington but there was no chance he could keep up the pace or the style further down. I flattened the accelerator and drew up beside him near the barracks; he glanced across at me and I thought he looked puzzled. He dropped off the speed a bit and I coat-of-painted him, sending the Merc screeching off half-left up the hill into Napier Street which is leafy and quiet.

He was a fast-reacting driver; he saw the barriers early and threw the car into a skidding, turning stop that tortured the steering and the tyres. He almost made it, too; but the right front light collapsed against a post and the engine stalled. I shoved the Falcon through a U-turn and jumped out. He was sitting bolt upright, staring straight ahead and fanning his sweating face with his hand. I yanked him out and half-carried him to my car. He struggled briefly and I almost broke his arm ramming him into the back seat. A few lights had gone on in the houses and I thought I could hear a siren in the distance. I got started and went into the maze of blocked-off and one-way streets until I thought it was safe to emerge and head for home.

I worried all the way back to Glebe about leaving him over the back with the .38 floating around somewhere, but he stayed still and quiet, apart from doing a bit of muttering and groaning. I hauled him into the house and stuck him under a shower while I made coffee. I had a quick whisky while the coffee brewed and felt pretty pleased with myself.

He came out with a towel wrapped around his thin hips and plopped down in a chair at the table. I poured him some coffee.

'Thanks.' He eyed the Scotch and I added a bit to his mug. He took a few sips, wiped some drops of water off his face and started to look a bit better.

'Who're you?' he said.

'Hardy, private investigator. Vance Hill hired me to find you.'

'That shit.' He drank noisily. 'Still, thanks, I'll just finish this and I'll be off.'

I shook my head. 'No, I'm delivering you to Hill.'

'Be buggered you are.' He half-rose from his chair but I reached over and pushed him back.

'Use your head. How did you like being strapped to the bed?'

'Not much,' he muttered. 'Why can't people leave me alone?'

'You've got what they want. Look, son, I don't want to heavy you but this needs straightening out.' I dug into my jeans pocket, pulled out Ro Bush's card and slapped it on the table. 'She's got your interests at heart hasn't she?'

'Ro? Sure.'

'We'll talk to her as well as Hill, don't worry. Gordon was trying to pinch your song, right?'

He finished his coffee and I poured some more along with whisky for both of us. His fingers were long, thin and strong, like Con's without the tobacco stains. He looked tired and washed-out. A bit of a talk, another Scotch and I was pretty sure he'd sleep for ten hours.

'The song, yeah. Shit, I wish I'd never written the fuckin' thing.'

'You did write it, did you?'

'Bloody oath. Sport's shitting himself. You saw all that crap he's got—swimming pool and all? He's got debts up to here. Solo, he's shit.'

'How much did he get out of you?'

'Bugger all.' He grinned showing surprisingly good teeth. 'I just couldn't remember how it went. God, I'm tired.'

I put him in the spare room and locked the door,

but he was still asleep when I woke up. We walked to Annandale through the cool morning air and he filled me in a bit more on what had happened. He'd done some drinking and dope smoking after he'd stormed out of the studio, but nothing hard. Gordon picked him up a few days later, got him drunk and made him the prisoner of Bellevue Hill.

'Wouldn't be the first time a song changed hands for a bottle. Or some smack. That'd have been the next thing.' He whistled tunefully and grinned at me. 'I'd had a lot of bourbon and practically no sleep when you barged in. I just saw the door and went. Wonder what Sport'll do about the Merc? Probably owes a bundle on it.'

Ro Bush and Hill greeted Talbot as if he was Mick Jagger who'd just dropped by with his band to help out. He disappeared into the studio and I was left with Hill and the sordid business of my cheque. He signed with a flourish and handed it over.

'Good job, thanks.'

'Better keep an eye on him.'

'Will do.'

'Will he get his way with the production of the song?'

His eyes narrowed and all the money-worry lines on his face deepened. 'Maybe.'

I heard the song when it came out; there was a different singer, less chorus and more mandolin, but it still lacked the nice, light beat I'd liked and sounded like bricks being dropped on a tin roof. I despaired for the younger generation, but then, so had my Dad when I got my first pair of pegged pants.

The Big Pinch

I felt a pang, I won't deny it, when I yanked out the pin that held the card to the door. I crumpled the card and put it in my pocket, closed the door. CLIFF HARDY—PRIVATE INVESTIGATIONS was out of business. As I went down the corridor, past the voice teacher and the horoscope-caster, I tried to remember how much turnover there'd been along that corridor in the twelve years I'd graced it with my office. A lot, and now my turn had come. I didn't imagine it was any different from the experience of the guitar teacher and the graphic artist and the literary agent—just a matter of the door opening too many times for the occupant and not enough times for clients.

I could have paid the rent for another month; hell, the rent was *paid* a couple of weeks in advance, but there didn't seem to be any point in just sitting there listening to my hair grow. *Get out, Cliff*, I could hear a voice saying. *Don't wait until you can't pay the rent—retire with the title*.

I tried a little Gene Kelly dance on the stairs, telling myself that it would be a relief to go to work for the Roger Wallace Agency—to get a salary cheque and be insured against breakage. A company car maybe. Eight steps down I lost balance and would have fallen if a man coming up hadn't steadied me. His grip on my arm was firm; I felt embarrassed and more so that he knew me.

'Mr Hardy? Been watching *Flashdance*?'

'No, just young and foolish. Do I know you?'

'We've never met but you were described to me. I want to hire you; that is, if you're not all tied up at Arthur Murray's.' He was a dark, smooth-featured man, a little shorter and wider than me and he smelled of expensive after-shave when he pushed his smooth face close to my rough one.

'What's the idea?' I jerked my arm free.

'I wanted to see if you'd been drinking.'

'I don't drink before six these days.' As I said it I was thinking that today might be an exception.

'So I've heard, that's good. Can we talk business?'

What could I do? He looked, smelt and moved like money, and a flash company car would only get vandalised in my street, anyway. Still, I nearly reverted to my previous decision when I found out that he was in the movie business. He leaned forward and rested his elbows in the dust on my desk, laced his fingers under his chin and talked. It sounds uncomfortable but it's actually not a bad talking posture; it gave him a forward-thrusting, determined look.

'My company starts shooting today, this afternoon. That's Boston Picture, we ...'

'Boston?'

'Just a name, we're making ...'

'Why not Brisbane Pictures, Mr Boston?'

He sighed. 'I was told you had a sense of humour. I suppose this is it. My name is Fuller, Richard Fuller. I'm the executive producer of a movie called *Death Feast*.'

'I haven't read the book.'

'It's not that sort of picture, there hasn't been a book, there never will be a book—not even a novelisation. Trouble is, there mightn't be a picture unless I can get this wrinkle ironed out.'

I like a good command of metaphor; I nodded and

shut up and let Fuller smoke his cigarettes in a tar-guard-holder and tell it the way he wanted to.

'*Death Feast* is an action picture, sort of cops'n robbers thing set in Sydney, Kurt Butler's the star. The script is better than average, we've got great locations and a terrific crew.' He drew deeply on his low tar, filtered, tar-guarded cigarette and filled his lungs luxuriously. 'We've also got a TV pre-sale. Big one. You know what that means?'

'I suppose the picture has a chance of coming out ahead.'

'Has to. Can't help it.' He expelled the smoke and took in some more. 'If the bloody thing ever gets shot. Some crank's threatened Kurt's wife; he wanted to pull out, take her to Acapulco or some damned place. I promised I'd handle it, make him happy. You're the solution we came up with.'

'Why not delay the thing? Check on the crank, grab him or wait till he stops?'

He shook his head. 'We've got non-completion clauses, other people are tied up later, weather problems—it's now or never.'

'How long's the shooting last?'

'Six weeks.'

'I charge a hundred and twenty-five dollars a day—you're looking at five thousand bucks.'

'We've got a 2.3 million budget, as a below the line cost it's a piddle in the bay.'

'Where's the wife going to be? There'll be a big expense sheet if I have to hang around Palm Beach renting speedboats.'

'She'll be on the set every day, she always is. Kurt doesn't comb his hair without asking her first.'

'Is that why the crank's working on her—to get at him?'

'I hadn't thought of it.'

'Who's handling the crank angle—looking into that?'

'No one, that's another problem. I'll pay you a hundred and fifty a day; no, let's say a hundred and seventy-five.'

'What for?'

He looked nervous for the first time, maybe for the first time in his life. 'You won't like it. Kurt plays a private eye in the film. He thinks it will help his performance if he can sort of assist you in your investigation of the crank calls.'

'I'm investigating them, am I? Not just guarding the wife?'

'Hell, the set'll be bristling with security men, she'll be as safe as houses.'

I squinted against a ball of light that came in the window and bounced off the metal filing cabinet behind Fuller.

'You didn't exactly play that very straight, did you?'

He grinned. 'Sort of sideways.'

'I expected a better metaphor.' He looked puzzled and I slammed down the front legs of the chair I'd been leaning back in. 'Skip it. Write me a below-the-line cheque, show me how generous you are.'

It was generous enough to make me forget about guitar teachers and rent and Roger Wallace.

I followed Fuller's new Commodore in my old Falcon to Leichhardt where the interior scenes of the movie were to be shot. He stopped in front of a terrace house in one of the narrower streets and a plane roared overhead as we stood outside the place. He spoke but the jet noise drowned him out and I leaned my head towards him.

'Hear that?' he said. 'That's what we wanted—great dramatic effect.'

'Yeah,' I said. 'It'll cut down on the dialogue.'

'Always a plus. Come and meet the mad house.'

I followed him into the house which looked as if a

giant metal arm had ripped out all the walls and half the ceiling. The rooms seemed to have been dismembered, and the floor crawled with black power leads. There were forests of light stands and boom microphones and clusters of cameras that looked to be talking to each other. There wasn't a canvas-backed chair in sight, but a group of people were squatting on a few uncluttered square inches of floor and one had a rolled up manuscript in his hand and was thumping the boards with it. If he wasn't the director the film was in trouble already.

'Scene conference,' Fuller whispered. 'Better not disturb them. Coffee?'

I shook my head; drinking coffee in the morning makes me want to drink wine in the afternoon. 'Fill me in on the people.'

'Okay. Kurt you'll know; the guy with the script is Iain Mcleish, he's directing it; the little man with the hair is Bob Space, the writer; the other guy is Josh Wild, he's an actor, and the blonde is Jardie, Kurt's wife.'

'I bet her Mum never called her Jardie.'

'Her Mum would've called her Boss, like everyone else. Look at her now!'

The small blonde woman with the tight curls and the tight pants was laying down the law to McLeish. Butler watched her indulgently: I'd seen him on television in one of his tough guy roles in which he'd spent a lot of time naked or nearly so; if you needed an actor with shoulders you couldn't go past him. Space, who couldn't have stood much above five foot but had another four inches of woolly hair on top of that, was nodding at Jardie Butler's every word. He wore sloppy old trousers and a faded army shirt and his feet were bare; as he nodded he scribbled notes in a reporter's pad. Wild just looked straight ahead of him and McLeish looked down at the floor, perhaps at Space's feet. Butler clapped his hands and his actor's voice boomed out across the technology-crammed room.

'Let's do it that way, sounds good. Let's get going!'

McLeish unsquatted and wandered off towards the back of the house. I heard his voice lift in a quick, angry Scots-accented shout.

Fuller and I picked our way across the snake pit.

'Kurt, this is Hardy, the guy we talked about.'

Butler shook my hand in a powerful grip that must've started in the shoulders.

'You agreeable?' he rumbled.

'We'll give it a try.'

'Good. C'mon Josh, let's get fixed up. Should have some time to talk to you this afternoon. Is that right, love?'

Mrs Butler looked up a foot or so; she had a small, pointed face that looked even sharper when inclined.

'Should be if that Scots twit is half as good as he thinks he is. I'll give Mr Hardy the details.'

Butler nodded and he and Wild disappeared behind some cameras. Fuller was looking relieved that Jardie Butler hadn't said I was too tall or the wrong colour. He slapped Bob Space on the shoulder and laughed.

'Know what this guy said, Bob, when I told him about the picture? He'd said he hadn't read the book! Good?'

Space blinked two or three times quickly and clenched his fists; for a moment he was sixty inches of pure aggression. Then he relaxed and let go a grin that showed his stained teeth.

'Hah, hah,' he said. 'The laconic Aussie wit we're famous for. D'you think you can get Kurt to be a bit warmer, Jardie, love—touch less craggy? We're supposed to like him.'

'How craggy should a private eye be, Mr Hardy?' She turned on me a pair of grey eyes that shone hard and cold, like a slate roof in the rain.

'It depends how smart he is,' I said. 'If you need some extra cragginess you can always hire it.'

She nodded. 'After Richard shows you the set-up I'll tell you about our problem.' She swung back to Space and moved him away with body language. 'Changes, sure,' she said. 'But not just for the sake of change, Bob. Constructive . . .'

I broke down and accepted a cup of coffee while Fuller gave me the tour. The company had taken over three adjoining houses and gutted the middle one. There were generators, refrigerators and fans all over the place. I counted fifteen telephones in the three houses. There were caravans in the biggest of the backyards and another couple in the laneway behind the houses.

'They're for the cast and some of the crew. I've got an office in one. Bob Space has a writing room in one.'

'Hasn't he finished the script?'

'There're always changes, sometimes it's handy to have the writer on deck. Space says he sees his script as fluid.'

'Piss!' McLeish was suddenly standing beside us. He seemed to have a higher colour than when I'd first seen him and he was sucking some kind of sweet. 'Script started off just fine, just fine, but between them the Butlers and Space are re-writing it by the hour. It's getting worse.'

'Shoot it your way, Iain, that's your job.'

'Aye,' McLeish said vaguely.

Butler and Wild were deep in conversation over a table covered with bottles and the crew was all packed around them, each man and woman performing some small, essential task. When Jardie

Butler was satisfied with the look of things she beckoned me to go out back with her. She cocked one leg in skin-tight red satin pants over a low brick wall, took a deep breath of the Leichhardt air and gave me one of her Boss looks. She was strongly built, with wide shoulders and a flattish chest; her sex appeal was in her strength and she seemed to know it.

'You're no oil painting,' she said. 'How old are you?'

'Around forty.'

'You look it. Kurt's twenty-five and looks thirty, I wonder what he'll look like at forty.'

'It'll depend on the lighting. Tell me about these crank calls.'

'They started about two weeks ago, no, three. Really weird stuff—like he said he'd throw acid in my face, or cut me. Said how would I look after I'd gone through a windscreen—stuff like that.'

'Anything actually happen?'

'No, but I've had a creepy feeling—like I'm being watched. It really got to Kurt.'

'Was that the idea d'you think? I mean, I suppose you could have enemies . . .'

She laughed. 'You mean I'm a domineering bitch. You're right, I am. I haven't got any talent you see, and a girl's got to make her way somehow.'

'I guess so. Well, I'll hang around. I suppose I can go for a drive with Kurt, talk to a few people where you live, check a few things out. I don't really think I can give him the flavour of the work though.'

'Humour him. It's just another *macho* fantasy.'

'I can't work out what you really think of him.'

She grinned and a little warmth showed in the slate eyes. 'Neither can I.'

They got through working, if that's what you'd call

it, by 7 o'clock. I heard McLeish say they might get two minutes out of it and that that wasn't too bad. Butler was too tired to do any sleuthing and I wound up my day by talking to the three security guards who'd be on duty all night. They weren't bright but they seemed to be able to grasp that they should pay special attention to the Butler caravan. The happy young couple lived at Whale Beach, so they were in temporary residence on the set.

There was a small drinking party in progress when I left. In one of the undeveloped kitchens Space, McLeish, two actresses and a crewman were working their way through some wine and whisky. They didn't invite me to join them so I went to where I keep my modest supplies of the same items.

The next day was one of the most boring I recall; I hung around the set while they ground out another two minutes. A copy of the script was lying around and I picked it up as a keepsake—from what I could see it was unlikely that I'd ever want to read it. I talked to Butler after he finished shooting and told him I'd check on whether there'd been any attempts to learn his unlisted number and invited him to go with me to do some snooping in Whale Beach.

'No way, man, I'd like to but I just can't make it. Bob's done these new scenes and I've got to look 'em over tonight. Tell you what, I'm going for a run tomorrow, early. What say you come with me—6 o'clock say. You can tell me how it went.'

I thought it'd give me a chance to see how the security boys were shaping up at first light and maybe Butler would have a few more ideas in his head at that time. I agreed to meet him on the street at six. There were three messages waiting for me at home—all prospective clients. I rang two of them and made appointments. I couldn't see myself spinning out the *Death Feast* job for six weeks and it seemed smart to take advantage of the sudden easing of my personal recession.

We had the run, and Butler couldn't resist keeping ahead of me and being more agile over the gutters. Leichhardt woke up around us; dogs yapped, and trucks delivered to shops and the cooking smells in the street suggested better breakfasts than tea and toast. I did a fair bit of panting as Butler showcased: we didn't talk much. The action started at around eleven when Jardie Butler knocked over a camera and punched a cameraman who swore at her. I moved in fast to break it up, and eased her away from the broken glass and the fuming technician.

'Easy, easy,' I said. 'What's the matter?'

'I got another one of those bloody calls! Right here, on the set!'

'Where's Kurt?'

'In the other house, getting made up. I didn't want him to hear about it until I'd seen you. Then I knocked over the stupid camera.'

'Same voice?'

'I think so, yes.'

'Describe it while it's fresh—what did he say?'

She shook slightly and I helped her to sit down on the steps of one of the caravans. 'He said, he said ". . . I'll wash your face for you, I'll wash it right off." Ugh. it's a sort of thin, reedy voice, high . . .'

I got some brandy for her, and then she showed me the phone in the end house where she'd taken the call. One of the daytime security men had called Jardie to the phone but he couldn't recall anything special about the voice. He scratched his ear under his aggressively cropped hair.

'Funny thing though, that's a closed line.'

'What d'you mean?' I snapped.

'You can only get that to ring by using one of the

other phones on the set. Why, what's up?'

Jardie Butler's hands flew to her face and she covered it like a little girl playing hidey. 'Jesus!'

'Who else'd know about the closed line?'

'I dunno. Other security blokes; the bloke that installed them, and ... ah, a couple of the ... what d'you call them? Assistants.'

'Okay, could you do a job for me? Just keep a watch and make a note of anyone who leaves this morning. Don't stop them—just get the name and the time. Right?'

Like me, he looked glad to be relieved of the boredom and he hurried off. I helped Jardie up and made her finish the brandy.

'We've got to do a quick tour, get to know everyone here. You know most of the names?'

'Most, not all.'

'Descriptions or jobs for the rest. Let's go.'

We prowled the three houses looking in doors and checking in toilets; when we finished we had a list of twenty-two names and eight physical and eleven job descriptions. All the principals were there: Butler, McLeish, Space, Wild and a gaggle of supporting players—there were technicians of various sorts, and other functionaries down to a kid who controlled car movement in the street and a cook. Jardie and I went through the list crossing out names of people who couldn't have made the call because they were definitely otherwise engaged at the time or because she could see them at the time of the call. Butler, McLeish and a big swag of the technicians went out; I removed myself from the list and the security man who'd told us about the phone. I was about to cross out the wardrobe woman when Jardie stopped me.

'What're you doing? Where was she?'

'She's a she—you said it was a man's voice.'

'I'm not sure now, it could have been disguised.'
'Christ, that opens it up.'
'What d'we do now? I'm impressed so far, by the way.'
'Thanks.'

She was wearing her tight pants in white today, with a singlet cut low under the arms. She had very nice slim arms with long muscles; it looked as if she exercised as much as Kurt. She moved with a dancer-like graceful confidence and she wouldn't normally have knocked over a camera. I was convinced that the phone call had been truly unpleasant.

'The person who made the call wouldn't have known that it was an internal-calls-only phone. He or she wouldn't be worried about anything and there's no reason to think they'd act any different from normal. I guess I'll just have to check on all the obvious people—the ones who might have a reason to sabotage the film.'

'That's no one,' Jardie muttered. 'Haven't you heard how things are in this business? Work's work.'

'Someone's got a reason, unless...'

'Unless what?'

'Someone who's *not* here who *does* have a reason hired someone who is here who doesn't.'

'Oh, great.'

From the other house Butler's voice rose in a shout that lifted the dust.

'I cannot work with that crazy bastard! What *is* the matter with him?'

It was a red alert to Jardie; she took off, scooting through the gap in the fence like a startled rabbit. I followed sedately and stepped into a madhouse: Butler, McLeish and Space were all shouting at each other simultaneously. Butler looked to be ready to use his fists on someone and McLeish had a bad, high colour with veins throbbing in his forehead. Space had more control and looked to be more excited than angry. Jardie pushed Space aside and he shut up and watched her go to work on Butler. Her technique was a combination of stick and carrot. She whacked him in the ribs to cut his breath and then stroked his arm like a vet with a frightened animal. Her touch seemed to calm him and he touched her in return. Maybe they'd done an advanced course in feelie therapy, because the touching seemed to do them both a lot of good.

McLeish ran out of steam and signalled to one of the young women whose function had never been clear to me. She ducked back and came up with a glass and a bottle of Haig, and that particular doubt was answered. McLeish took a stiff belt as his way of cutting *his* breath, poured another and sipped.

'Okay, okay,' he said quietly. 'We've got a wee problem.' He nodded to the whisky bearer. 'Get his agent on the phone, lass, we'll work it out.'

Space turned over script sheets rapidly. 'Guess I could change the lines, even write him out if need be.'

McLeish drained his glass in a one jerky swallow. 'Christ man, you'll be giving us a new bloody film the way you're going. You've got first feature jitters—relax. The sensible people'll work it out, I tell you. Take a break, everybody.'

'We know what that means for you,' Jardie snarled.

'Don't push me, girlie. You'll get your cans full of the sort of shit you want, don't you worry.'

He wandered off after the Haig bottle and I watched Butler pull on a sweatshirt over the T-shirt he'd been wearing for the scene. He seemed to approach his acting like an athletic event.

'What happened?' I asked.

'Wildy blew up.' Butler said. 'He's been acting crazy for days, from rehearsals on. I don't know what the hell's the matter with him. Now he's pissed off somewhere and this scene is shot to bits.'

'Take it easy,' Jardie said. 'Have some coffee, have a rest; Hardy and I'll go and get him.'

'I don't want you going around unprotected,' Butler said. 'Not after the threats.'

'What threats?' Space asked.

'Never mind, Bob. I am protected, you dummy.' Jardie stroked her husband's arm and gripped the bicep. 'I've got the guy we hired.'

'I thought you were some kind of technical consultant,' Space said. 'That's what Richard told me.'

'That's Richard's job. Go back to cutting scenes, Bob. Have a rest, hon. Let's go, Hardy.'

We went through the house and out to the street; the security man I'd assigned to plot the comings and goings rushed up.

'One of the actors took off,' he said excitedly. 'Burning rubber.'

'Thanks,' I said. 'Stay with it.'

Jardie Butler turned out to be an expert driver of her Stag. We were whipping down Norton Street before I had the seat belt buckled.

'I know where he lives—Balmain.'

'That right?'

'Yes. You might as well know, Josh and I had a bit of a thing before I met Kurt. Josh's not over it properly.'

'You think he could be the phone caller?'

'I suppose it's possible. See, he was all set to become the muscular hero of the 1980s before Kurt came along. Kurt got a couple of roles Josh thought he should've had. He's taken it bad—this is the first time he's agreed to work with Kurt.'

'Missed out on you too did he?'

'Sort of.'

'Could Wild have been the voice on the phone?'

She was heading along the railway to the intersection with the Crescent, too fast I thought, but she braked and made the turn neatly. 'He's an actor—who knows what actors can do . . . and can't do.'

I chewed on that for the rest of the drive down into east Balmain. Wild lived close to the wharf and the water but, he couldn't have seen either from the small windows of the nondescript block of 1950s flats—he might as well have been in Haberfield. Jardie U-turned and rolled the car to the kerb just short of the drive with the practised ease of someone who'd done it before.

We walked up the drive and she pointed to a Moke parked skew-whiff beside the flats.

'He's here—at the back.'

The narrow concrete porch at the back would barely have kept the rain off the peeling door of flat three. For an almost star, Josh Wild didn't appear to be doing too well. Jardie knocked and the door opened slowly. Wild's face began to move into a smile at the sight of her until he saw me. Then it changed and blurred like a double exposed photograph. The flat door opened inwards but the screen door opened out and Wild used it to knock Jardie Butler out of his path. He growled like an animal, reached out for me and pulled on the front of my shirt. I went with the pull; he had a punch ready but he'd advertised it much too early. I went under the punch and bullocked him back into the hallway. He swung again but he was badly off-balance and I hooked his feet out, and down he went.

Jardie's breathing was harsh in my ear as I stood

over her crumpled ex-lover. There was a trickle of blood from his mouth but he hadn't hit the wall or floor very hard and had no reason to be as relaxed as he was. I looked from him to her and couldn't decide which sight I disliked more.

'Wow!' she breathed. 'Is that how it's done?'

'It shouldn't be that easy, big bloke like him. Take a look—you know him—reckon he's okay?'

She brushed past me and leaned over Wild. All hunched up on the floor like that isn't a man's best posture, but with the thinning hair I could see now and the slack jaw muscles, it didn't look as if he could have been a film idol for long. His gut looked a bit slack too, but even so he shouldn't have been such a pushover.

Jardie straightened up. 'He's coked,' she said.

'You sure?'

'Seen it a hundred times, him and others, He'd be calm and relaxed in a hurricane, that's how it takes him. He couldn't fight coked to defend his mother—Kurt'd be like a chainsaw.'

I got Wild up in a sort of fireman's lift, carried him the few feet it took and dumped him on a battered narrow couch in the small, dark living room. I went out to the kitchen, wet a dirty dishtowel and slopped it over his face. He started to clean himself carefully with his eyes closed, like a cat. We ignored him.

'How come he lives so low on the pig? Don't actors make a good living?'

'I didn't realise he'd slid this far. I hate to think how much this stuff costs.' She was standing by a low coffee table which had a mirror on it and a plastic packet and a short straw with the end scoop-shaped.

'So he rushed off to make his connection here.' There was a dribble of saliva on the mirror, and some of the powder was smeared in it. 'I thought half the people in the acting game were on this stuff, does it turn them all into maniacs?'

'No, different people handle it different ways. Josh must've been really strung out. Maybe he's on something else too.'

'Would it make him screw up his part?'

'Christ, yes, it could. With Bob Space on the set though, it's a wonder he didn't write it in—make Josh a smack head.'

Wild's eyes were open and he was finished washing his face. I took the cloth away and he smiled at me. 'Everyone says that about Space, about him changing things. Isn't that standard?'

'Not quite. Look, Hardy, now I think about it I really don't think Josh could be the caller. I mean, he's a nut, and he probably still fancies me and maybe he hates Kurt. But he wouldn't wreck the film—especially not needing money that bad.'

'I suppose. Well, you talk to him and I'll poke around—look for clues.'

'To what?'

I shrugged. 'Who knows, I'm a snoop. You're a smart girl, you talk to him; if you decide he wouldn't threaten to throw acid in your face, I'll believe you.'

I could hear them murmuring as I searched Wild's bedroom and the other small room he used to store things—mostly rubbish. He wasn't a neat man or a clean one—he wasn't very interesting either. Like alcoholics I'd known, his life seemed to be given over to drugs: he had smoking and sniffing and injecting devices, old containers marked with the residue of one dream-maker or another. The few books around had a drugs bias too. I could imagine him, like the dipsos, mapping out the geography of his days in terms of his hits—the only difference being that his hits were illegal and much more expensive. When I went back into the living room Wild was sitting up on the couch and Jardie was holding his hand.

'You'd only be doing it for Kurt,' Wild was saying.

'What does it matter?' she said. She looked across at me. 'Not him—no chance.'

'Okay.'

'You take the Moke back to the set, the keys're over there. I'll bring him along in a while. Tell them everything is okay.'

I collected the keys and had all the fun of jarring my spine with my hair in my eyes as I drove the Moke back to Leichhardt.

A kind of defeated calm had settled on the three houses. I strolled past the car control kid and tossed him the keys.

'He'll be along in a bit.'

The kid's jaw dropped and he looked at me as if I was Michael Jackson. *Cheap trick, Hardy*, I thought; but then, few jaws drop for me. I located Fuller and gave him the good news; he sent someone off to find someone to tell McLeish that he could go back to work

'If he's not too drunk,' Fuller said. 'Sometimes I wonder why I'm not making floppy discs or something—too many crazies in this business.'

'We still haven't found our chief crazy. How important is this picture to you? Financially, I mean.'

'Bloody important. Why?'

'That lets you out as a candidate for the phone caller; that is, if you're not lying.'

'Jesus, Hardy, don't joke about it.'

'There has to be someone who comes out better if the picture gets stopped, or delayed—who?'

'No one.' Fuller lit a cigarette to help him think. 'I

lose my shirt; Kurt misses out on a good role and they're not so easy to come by; McLeish needs a commercial success for obvious reasons; Space wants the credit and he's got points if we go into the black. Also I haven't paid him for the property yet; if we don't make the picture he'll have to join the list of creditors and that'll be long, believe me. The assistant cameraman wants to be cameraman, the wardrobe girl wants to be in casting—everybody wants to move up. Everybody needs *Death Feast*.'

McLeish stepped through the fence looking spruce, too spruce. 'Hey ho,' he sang. 'I hear the errant son returns, let's be having you all.'

'He's drunk,' I said.

'He's a good director when he's paralytic, he used to be a great director when he was just pissed. He'll do.'

'What about all these women around? Could one of them have the hots for Kurt and be cutting up rough?'

Fuller smiled. 'No way, Kurt's not like that.'

'He's not?'

'Don't get me wrong.' He leaned towards me with male conspiratoriality. 'He's not gay or anything. He's just not very . . . active. Knew a girl who knew him—she reckoned he had all the sex drive of an old sofa.'

'Amazing.'

People started emerging from all points around the houses like ants coming out of holes. A sharp squeal of brakes outside announced Jardie and Wild's return, and within minutes they were all making up like mad and things started to hum. Fuller charged around for a while and then settled down to talk on the phone. I broke resolution again and had a beer from one of the fridges. The security man told me only two other people had left since Wild, and neither was a candidate for star billing. I watched them shoot a scene and saw the sweat dribbling off Butler after the eighth take. Wild was slow and had to be hurried through his lines; Space looked edgy, and spoiled one take by making a noise flapping the script. Jardie squatted just out of camera range and offered Butler massive support with her eyes and hands. He lapped it up. I decided I'd rather make the tea than act, write or direct.

Fuller put down the phone and beckoned me over; he was smiling.

'Good news from the distributors,' he said.

'Does that mean my cheque won't bounce?'

'You don't know how true you speak. No, everything should be all right now.'

'How many people are actually sleeping here, say tonight?'

'Let's see. McLeish, Kurt and Jardie; Roxie and Heathcliff ...'

'Heathcliff?'

'Heathcliff Hathaway, one of the support actors.'

'Will he ever get to be star with a name like Heathcliff?'

'With his talent, anything's possible.'

'He's got talent?'

'None. Bob Space tells me he's moved his things in for a bit ... if you're planning something boring like gathering everyone together for a rap session it won't work, not tonight anyway.'

'I wasn't, but why wouldn't it work?'

'There's a dinner on tonight at EJs, everyone's going. What are you planning?'

'Something sneaky,' I said.

It's my belief that when you find out someone's secrets, you find out what they are. Someone with no secrets may be what they seem—few are. I went back to Glebe the way homeowners do, to make sure it hadn't burned down or had the doors stolen; but, by 9 o'clock I was back in Leichhardt, wording up the security men to let me poke around for a while.

I did McLeish's caravan first; it bore all the signs of being occupied by a sort of filmic hit man. He was here to do a job and he'd brought enough clothes and enough money and the booze he could get on the spot. He might have a full life back in the old Dart, complete with photos of the wife and dog, but here he was just passing through. There were some uncomplimentary remarks scrawled on a copy of the script, a bit of correspondence with his agent about fees and a cupboard full of hangover remedies. His passport photograph was of a younger, more hopeful man.

Jardie Butler had trouble sleeping; she kept her Mogadon close to hand; there was a pile of books by the bed of the kind that poor sleepers flip through—short stories, pop biographies and Woody Allen scripts. There was also an eye mask and a vibrator. The Butlers had a lot of casual clothes and a lot of casual money; two passbook accounts were healthy, as were a keycard account and a building society deposit. They'd also left carelessly lying around the kind of money I usually count, fold and put carefully in my wallet.

Kurt Butler's effects included weights, running gear, a chest expander, various liniments and more jockstraps than socks. His only reading matter was a carefully kept scrapbook about his very favourite film actor. He had a copy of Space's script with his lines heavily underscored; there had been some editing done in Jardie's hand—all to make the speeches shorter.

Space's part of the caravan he shared with one

of the technicians was a crazy jumble of books, papers, credit cards and clothes. He seemed to have no ability to keep things in separate compartments: he had pipe tobacco in a cup, ball point pens in a shoe, and razor blades in with a packet of tea bags. Under his bunk though was a locked metal box. I teased it open with a piece of wire and found a book inside which had been carefully wrapped in tissue paper, like a Shakespeare first folio.

The book was a paperback, published twelve years before by MacRobertson & MacRobertson. It was the first in a mystery and adventure series, and I vaguely remembered the fanfare of announcement at the time. Entitled *Death Games* it was written by Deryck Hyclef and told the story of a private detective who had three clients in succession murdered. It seemed like a faster way to go out of business than the slow grind of the recession. I had my souvenired copy of Bob Space's script in my pocket and I sat down on his bunk and compared the two pieces of writing. Even with name changed (and he hadn't bothered to change them that much—Dirk Balfour becoming Dick Balmain for example), it was easy to see that *Death Feast* was a direct pinch.

There was no mention of Hyclef on the script, in fact it was called 'an original screenplay'. Space had tried a few minor plot changes but, without knowing anything about film editing, it seemed to me that if the cutter of the film wanted a backbone he'd end up with a plot very like that of Hyclef's book. In any case, the book was underlined and annotated in Space's writing. I rummaged in the mess and found an earlier draft of the script which included passages virtually transcribed from *Death Games*. If the Scriptwriter's Guild, of which he was a fully paid-up member, had any teeth, Mr Robert Space would have a very bloody neck.

I telephoned EJs to ensure that Fuller would come to the set rather than slope off to his penthouse; then I got a bottle from McLeish's caravan and the security boys and I had a few belts and swapped stories. I told them the one about the amusement park that had a ferris wheel stolen and they told me the one about the drunk who went to sleep on wet cement.

Fuller and Space turned up around midnight; the writer was drunk and unsteady, and his face seemed to dissolve when I laid the book in front of him. We were in the kitchen of one of the houses, and I got him a glass of water. I put the script down beside the book and didn't say anything. Space gulped the water and looked miserable.

'What's going on?' Fuller said.

'Bob pinched the story from this book. He pinched the characters, atmosphere, the lot.'

'Jesus,' Fuller breathed. 'Anything to drink besides water?'

We got McLeish's bottle and I poured two drinks, leaving Space with more water.

'Let's hear it, Bob,' I said.

Space sipped water and a little dribbled down his chin; he'd been running his hands through his highrise hair, flattening it and making him look more normal, younger and afraid. 'I didn't think the thing'd get to production. I was just after the development dough, thought I might get a first draft fee from some producer, you know.'

Fuller nodded.

'Well, it all took off. It moved too fast for me—suddenly it was final draft and then we were in pre-production. I didn't know what to do. I wouldn't really have hurt Jardie, you know that.'

I nodded this time.

'I just wanted to stop the bloody thing. I tried to

make a lot of changes but Jardie and McLeish blocked a lot of them. If we make it like this,' he tapped the script, 'someone'll spot it for sure. It'll be the finish of me.' He mustered a little spirit and looked at Fuller. 'You too, probably,' he said.

I drank some of McLeish's good whisky and thought about it. Space was flicking through the book. There was a picture of the author on the back cover—he looked youngish, thin and thoughtful.

'Why didn't you get on to this Hyclef bloke? Do some sort of deal with him?'

'I thought of that,' Space said. 'I gave it a try; but the firm went out of business. I asked around but no one'd ever heard of Hyclef. It could've been a pseudonym. I don't know.'

Fuller was sinking whisky and looking desperate; he could see his investment slipping away. I let it slip a little, and then cleared my throat noisily.

'Missing persons is one of my specialities.'

Fuller took the biggest punt of his life, and they went on with the shoot while I looked for Hyclef. I found him teaching at a school out from Broken Hill. He'd never had another word published—the collapse of MacRobertsons had hit him for six. He was a nice, naive man, disappointed in his thirties. He was thrilled with the deal Fuller and Space worked out with him for the film 'based on' his novel. There was talk of a re-issue of the book by another house with Kurt Butler's craggy features on the cover.

The film finished on schedule, and just over budget. It did good business and they even found a small part for me—I'm the one who shouts 'Look out!' when Dick Balmain misses death by inches up in the Centrepoint tower.

Maltese Falcon

It was warm for March in San Francisco they told me, and Dan Swan was sweating like a fat man on a bicycle, except he was a thin man, standing still. It wasn't surprising though; the group of twenty or so people clustered around him had on T-shirts and jeans, shorts or light slacks. Swan was wearing a shirt and tie, trench coat and heavy rubber-soled shoes. He had to dress like that. He had to wear the fedora too, he was taking us on his famous 'Sam Spade walking tour' through the Tenderloin and adjacent parts of San Francisco.

'We don't know much about Spade,' Swan said. 'My guess is he was born in Oregon or Washington State. He served in the infantry in World War One and was an NCO. Not high-ranked, a corporal, maybe.' He took off his hat and wiped his high brow which was getting higher as the widow's peak was accentuated by retreating hair on both sides. Dark hair and dark eyes, a long face and body. He moved his shoulders uncomfortably in the coat and I wanted to tell him to take it off.

'Where's the dingus?' A heavy guy in a floral shirt and floppy shorts spoke up at the front of the group. He held some money in his hand and he thrust it back into a pocket.

'I wanna see the bird,' he said.

Swan looked embarrassed. He wiped his face which was flushed now and not just from the heat. 'I haven't got it today,' he said. 'Too hot.'

That seemed fair enough to me. I was carrying a tourist guide too thick to go in my jeans pocket, and it felt too hot to carry that. Still, the promotion photo for the tour showed Swan sneaking down a street with a bundle wrapped in frayed newspaper under his arm, and if that was one of the things you wanted . . .

'This is a gyp,' the fat man grumbled. He took the steps back down to Larkin Street two at a time, and a fat woman, also in Bermuda shorts, followed him. After a pause, a thin, nervous looking woman in a print frock went down the steps and moved off in the other direction from the fat pair.

'Anyone else?' Swan was aggressive now, not bothering to exert charm. 'All right. I'll take the money—four dollars a head, two fifty for senior citizens.'

We all pressed forward with our money, serious takers. Swan collected his hundred dollars or so and told us a little more about Hammett and Spade.

'. . . the same skyline, post-earthquake, Spade would have seen. Let's take a look.' He almost sprinted down the steps from the Public Library and across the street, timing the lights just exactly right.

We skipped and lumbered and strode after him and got Dan's spiel about Spade defying the DA and then we headed off along the streets the Continental Op and the Whoosis Kid and Spade had haunted. The sun was high and Swan's fedora must have been welcome. He got more cheerful and answered some of the ignorant questions amiably as we went along. I caught him up at the corner of Geary and Leavenworth.

'What's the bird weigh?' I said innocently.

He gave me a sharp look. 'Where you from?'

'Australia, you know, where Hammett nearly went.'

'Yeah,' He grinned. 'It was a tough break.'

I stuck out my hand. 'Cliff Hardy. I'm in this line of work at home.'

We shook. 'Tours?' he said.

'No, detective work.'

He seemed a bit pre-occupied for the next hour while we traced Spade and Cairo and the others through the streets. He took us to a lane where you could see the faded name of a restaurant where Spade had eaten a steak. The building now housed a computer games outfit. Swan drew me aside.

'Bird weighs next to nothing,' he said. 'Couple of pounds.'

'Pretty light.'

'Yeah, aluminum. I haven't got it because it was stolen.'

Before I could say anything, a plastic bag filled with water came sailing down and burst on the sidewalk in the middle of the group. The water sprayed, picked up dust, and dirtied the clothes of a couple of women. Strong men swore. Then some garbage came down plus a couple of cans and those with combat experience ducked for cover. I saw a flash of face and the arc of an arm on top of the computer games building. I pointed up there to Swan.

He nodded tiredly. 'Not the first time.'

A couple of people started to walk away.

'You can have your money back!' Swan yelled.

One of the men bent, picked up a can and threw it at Swan. It was a light toss, but Swan wasn't prepared. I was, I stepped forward and caught the can. I thought of throwing it back but remembered that I was a stranger in a strange land. I threw the can into a trash bin.

'Thanks,' Swan said. 'This goes on, and I'm out of business.'

He rushed through the rest of the tour and wasn't helped by the inattention of the clients who looked up every time we stopped. He signed off on Market Street, and signalled me to wait while he autographed a few copies of his tour booklet for the faithful.

'Drink?' he said when he was through.

We had been out on the hot streets for almost four hours, a drink didn't seem like too much of an indulgence. Swan led the way to a quiet bar and ordered two beers without consulting me.

'All Aussies drink beer,' he said when the waiter arrived with two big bottles of Budweiser, glasses and peanuts.

'Some drink absinthe,' I said.

'No kidding?'

Budweiser is good beer and so is Coors and Schlitz and every other one I'd tasted in California. We drank some of it and I waited for him to say whatever it was the beer had been bought for.

'Ah ... this is kinda embarrassing. You know, I'm supposed to be well up on all this detective stuff.'

'But you're not. And somebody stole your bird?'

'Right. And there's more. The shop's in trouble—that's the Bay Mystery Bookstore on O'Farrell Street, you know it?'

I shook my head.

'Well, I run it and it's done okay until lately. Then the bird goes missing, plus we get that crap from the roof. I feel like a target. I feel like somebody's out to get me.'

'Who would be?'

He scratched his heavily stubbled chin and pulled

out a packet of cigarillos. 'You smoke, Hardy?'

'I quit.'

'Stay with it.' He lit up and took a pull of beer. 'I suppose there could be someone wanting to muscle in on this tour racket. I was the first to do it, but anyone could who had the knowledge and that's in the books.'

'How much d'you make at it?'

'In a big week, three or four tours, I might make four hundred bucks. Wouldn't average nearly that, though.'

I considered it. 'It's not a lot to break the law for. Besides, you've got the book published, it's your baby. What else—the shop, women, drugs?'

He shook his head. 'Store does okay like I said, nothing spectacular. I'm between women just now, leastways I hope I am. Nothing there.' He swished beer in his glass and puffed smoke. 'These are the only drugs I use.'

'Why did you say you were embarrassed?'

'I need help. I'd get laughed away if I went to any of the investigators in this city. Straight to the press. Somebody stole my Maltese Falcon—shit!'

'The police?'

'What crime? Fuckin' bird's worth maybe fifty dollars. Harassment? I'm not sure there is such a crime. Cops've got work to do, rackets to run, you know.'

'Yeah. Politics?'

He fiddled with the fedora on the table; the band had a tiny feather in it and I was reminded of the hat my father always wore out of doors, hail, rain or shine. 'I used to think Tom Hayden was a good guy,' Swan said, 'now I hear he's spending a million bucks to prove he's not a radical. That's politics.'

I nodded. 'I was going home but I guess I can stay awhile. You're hiring me are you?'

194

He pulled his tour money out of the trench coat. 'What're your rates?'

'I get one hundred and twenty-five a day and expenses back home.'

He put the crumpled notes down in front of me. 'Be more than that here. Let's make it that *per diem*.'

I took the money. 'I'll look into it, give it a day or two. It's not my territory, I don't want to rip you off.'

He imitated my accent. 'Fair enough.'

'At least you didn't call me digger.' I forked out a ten. 'Let's do some more drinking.'

Swan had told me that he had two people working in his bookstore: a young woman named Maggie Bolton who worked part-time, and one Roger Milton-Smith who acted as manager when Swan was doing other things. I'm a nasty, suspicious character, if someone in trouble tells me his only associate is his mother I'll take a look at Mom.

According to Swan, Bolton would be in the shop that afternoon, Sunday being quiet, and she would knock off at 8 p.m. It was after six when we finished drinking and I told him I'd go back to my hotel for a shower and start work at eight.

'Doing what?' He drained his glass and the waiter came to take away his fourth bottle of Bud.

'Following Bolton,' I said.

I was staying in a cheap hotel on Sutter Street because I figured that all I needed was the room. I had a small transistor radio, I could watch the fights on the TV in the lounge and I've never minded walking a few metres to the bathroom. I had a big jug of Taylor's burgundy for companionship and I felt I was nicely set up for the few days I intended to spend in San Francisco seeing the sights.

It was a comfortable bed too, and I spent longer on it than I intended, so I was late getting to O'Farrell Street. I located the bookstore. Almost immediately its lights went off and a slim, red-headed woman stepped out. She gave the door a slam and a shake and set off down the street.

I followed her down Stockton and Fourth to the SPT Company depot. She was young and fit and she walked fast, passing a big bargain basement bookstore without a glance. Her mind wasn't on books. Innocently, I stood behind her while she bought a ticket to Burlingame and I did the same.

The train ride was all right, as train rides go in the dark. I wished I'd brought *The Hotel New Hampshire* with me from my room. Maggie Bolton read, or looked at, a fashion magazine with pictures of hollow-cheeked models on the back and front covers. She was pretty hollow-cheeked herself come to think of it, with a long, lean shape. She looked at the magazine as if she was making comparisons between the models and herself. Fair enough. I wondered why she hadn't taken a bus, which would have given me more to look at, and I found out why in Burlingame.

We got off the train, went through the gate and Bolton waited while a north-bound train pulled in. A tall blonde woman in a stylish pants suit got down and trotted forward on high heels. She and Bolton embraced on the sidewalk. They kissed and hung on for a bit and then started to walk arm in arm north along Rawlins road, talking animatedly. They stopped at a corner market and bought a jug of red wine and some french bread. I bought some bread too and some bananas and *Sports Illustrated*. Just short of the San Francisco city limits, the two women went into a modern apartment block. I circled it and saw a light go on three floors up that was probably theirs.

There was a pocket handkerchief sized park across from the apartments and I sat on a bench and ate half of the loaf and two bananas and read about John Elway of Stanford's tough decision whether to play pro football or baseball. I had to squint to read, but I could see the lights in the apartment go out in one room, go on in another, dim there for a while and then go on as before.

The first visitor arrived a little after ten in a taxi. A small Latin went into the building and there was a little action with the lights up on the third. He came out about twenty minutes later. Then a Ford Bronco with all the trimmings parked just around the corner and two bulky middle-aged men went in. Two dim lights for almost an hour. I read a piece about Jim Thorpe. Traffic was light on the street, but when I saw a police car cruising up I sauntered over to a bin to drop the magazine. The cops went past and when I got back to my bench a black man in a white suit was sitting on it. The jacket of the suit was double-breasted and so was the vest. He had a pencil line moustache and very neat, short hair.

'Nice night,' he said. He pushed my paper bag so that half a loaf of french bread and two bananas fell on the ground.

'Yes,' I said. 'It sure is.'

He grinned and made an ear trumpet with one hand. 'What do I hear? This the kinda food you eat over in England?'

'Yes. It sure is.'

'My. And I thought it was fish an' chee-ips.'

'That's the south.'

'Why're you watchin' number twelve, man?'

I sketched something Beardsleyesque in the air. 'Well, you know. Just trying to decide.'

He stood up. It struck me that he looked very like

Sugar Ray Robinson in his prime. 'Fish or cut bait.' he said.

I cut bait, but I picked up my bread and bananas first.

Back at the hotel I finished the bread and the Irving book and had some burgundy to wash them down. Maggie Bolton was in love, gainfully employed and her Pimp's suit cost ten times the value of the Maltese Falcon. It was hard to see either of them bothering.

In the morning I called Swan and gave him the news.

'A whore?', he said, 'Maggie?'

'If she's a tall red head with legs.'

'She is. I don't know what to say.'

'Can I come over and look around—where you kept the bird and all?'

'Sure. Store's not open till twelve.'

'Why's that?'

'Market research. People don't buy mysteries in the morning. You can come up to my place, though. I live here. There's a door in the alley.'

'Milton-Smith around yet?'

'No.'

'Good.'

The bookshop went in for Bogartiana, Christieana, Stoutiana and all the rest of it. The front window had a first edition of *The Maltese Falcon* in a glass case, surrounded by Hammett, Chandler and Mac-Donald paperbacks. Maybe 20 per cent of the window display was given over to science fiction books. I averted my eyes from them and went down the alley.

I knocked on a faded wooden door and heard fast steps clattering on wood inside. Swan opened the door with a beer can in his hand.

'Ascend,' he said.

The door led into a sort of storeroom at the back of the shop; it was full of cartons and discarded wrapping and packing paper lay around knee deep. Steep steps not much wider than a ladder led up to a loft above the shop. The one room contained a double mattress, table, sink, TV set, some cupboards and a refrigerator, but was basically given over to books. They covered most of the available wall space and lay in piles on the floor.

'Stock or personal?' I said.

He shrugged and made a half-and-half gesture. He tilted his can. 'Beer?'

'No thanks. Where'd you keep it?'

A heap of books had collapsed just near the top of the steps. He nudged them with his foot.

'Right here.'

I went down the steps and came up. I could reach the spot by leaning forward, not getting closer than a body length to the room. I jigged—no creaking.

'I thought at least it'd have to be lassoed through a window.'

He grinned. 'Shit, it's insured. It's the aggravation I'm worried about. You don't figure Maggie huh?'

I shook my head and prowled around the loft. The bed was neatly made, a few dishes were stacked by the sink. The windows were clean and overlooked O'Farrell Street. The sky was blue but there was some grey cloud out over the Bay. Swan pointed at it.

'Rain. And I've got a tour today. All I need is rain.'

I went over everything I could think of with him—the lease on the building, competitors in the Hammett and book business, friends with senses of humour—nothing. Just before noon I had a beer, and as some noises began to drift up from below, a ray of sunshine cut through the window.

'Maybe it won't rain,' Swan said shrugging into his trench coat. 'Store's open, want me to introduce you to Milt?'

'No,' I said. 'I'll just drift in like a customer.'

'Okay. Jesus, I feel naked without the bird.'

We went out to the alley and he headed off to the Town Hall to pick up his tourists. I walked around to the front of the shop and pushed open the door which had the famous thin man photograph of Hammett, blown up to poster size, stuck to the inside.

The bookstore was like a cross between a junkyard and a library. The walls had books floor to ceiling with sliding ladders attached to the shelves. There were books on tables and in free-standing bookshelves. There were books and comics and magazines in bins and boxes. It was disorderly, paperbacks mixed with hardcovers and leaves were as likely to be facing outwards as spines.

But one corner of the big room was tidy. It had the best light through a high window and was handy to the clerk's desk and the cash register. It had a big, neatly printed sign hanging over a geometrically arranged table of glossy hardcovers—SCIENCE FICTION & FANTASY.

I drifted around checking this and that and resisting the impulse to straighten things up a little. In the Sci-Fi section a man was doing just that. He was small and pot-bellied with thin, sandy hair brushed across a pink, mottled skull. He moved books from a table to the floor, expanding the section. He dealt enthusiastically with customers for the fantasy corner, less so with others.

Maybe it was just that he was busy with the little green men, maybe he wasn't really there at all, but he didn't seem to notice the shoplifter who carried out an armful of books with a technique that could only be called brazen.

I selected a Robert B. Parker paperback and went up to the register.

'I'll take this, please.'

He grunted.

'He's good isn't he, Parker?'

Another grunt. He rang it up and gave me change out of five.

'Have you got *A Canticle for Leibowitz*?'

He brightened visibly. His pudgy hands clasped in a fleeting attitude of reverence. 'No, we're out of it right now, but I could get it in for you. If you'd like to leave your name and number?' He pounced on a scribbling pad and pen, whipped them down in front of me. I wrote John Watson and my Sydney telephone number and left after thanking him.

It didn't rain. I hung around looking in windows and watching the store. I bought a take-out coffee and drank it sitting on the bus stop seat opposite the store. When I dropped the container into a rubbish bin I looked inside for no good reason. I don't think much of John D. MacDonald but I didn't see why a brand new copy of his latest book should be sitting in the bottom of a rubbish bin. Along with it was a book about Agatha Christie by Robert Barnard, a Lew Archer omnibus and a fat biography of James M. Cain. I retrieved the books and went off to catch up with Swan on Market Street.

'Any garbage today?' I asked him.

'Sure, same place. Came pelting down.'

I showed him the books and told him about how his 2IC ran the depot.

'Well,' he said, 'Milt's hot for all that shit. He persuaded me to include a section and it's done okay.'

'I'm not surprised, he runs it like Tiffany's.'

201

Swan hefted the books in his hands. 'This is bad, maybe Milt's eyesight is shot.'

'He doesn't wear glasses. He could tell an Asimov from a Zelazny at a hundred metres. Could he be trying to take you over and open the Six Rings of Uranus bookstore and brainwash?'

He laughed. 'Milt? Come on?'

'I'll look into him just the same. When's the next tour?'

'Tomorrow. Why?'

'I fancy a rooftop view. When you're back at the shop act normal. Don't shoot the shoplifters.'

He said okay and gave me his day's takings again. I felt guilty grabbing the money he'd pounded the pavement and his tonsils for, but business is business. I went back to my hotel and read *Early Autumn*, in which Parker's PI, Spenser, taught a kid how to run, pump iron, build a house and drink beer, all of which would be useful to him in later life.

That night I followed Milton-Smith to a place on Washington Street in Chinatown which you got into by giving twenty dollars to an old woman who wove cane baskets on the doorstep. I played blackjack and lost ten or twelve dollars. Milt played poker and lost a lot more. He signed things and had a serious talk with a Chinese gentleman in an English suit.

Two o'clock the next afternoon saw me on top of the computer games building. I looked down into the lane where Swan was due in about twenty minutes. The rooftop was flat with a rail around it; getting up to the fire escape was child's play for a man who didn't smoke and had once cleared five foot eight in the high jump. I hid behind a big box housing the building's electrical system and waited.

He came ten minutes later: sneakers, jeans and jacket, knitted wool cap. At the roof edge he laid out the goodies from a supermarket sack—waterbag, tomatoes, a soggy-looking parcel wrapped in newspaper.

I stepped out and cleared my throat. 'Conspiracy to litter,' I said. 'Ninety days.'

He spun around and I recognised him as the shoplifter. I took a couple of steps and he backed to the rail.

'Shoplifting, too.'

He threw a slow right when I was out of range, and I stepped inside it and clipped him with my left. A fighter he wasn't, he tripped on his own feet and flipped back over the rail. I jumped and grabbed his arm while his feet clawed at the sheer brick wall.

'Oh, Jesus,' he sobbed. 'Oh, Jesus.'

His jacket had a slick surface and I could feel my grip slipping.

'Swing your arm up and grab the edge.'

He said something about Jesus again but he got three fingers over the edge. I reached down, grabbed his jacket and belt and hauled him back up under the rail like a net full of fish. The jacket tore and slipped up his back and off as he scraped skin from his fingers getting a hold.

I was lying prone on the roof and gasping when I saw Swan come into the lane with his group. There was heavy breathing behind me, a sound like a knuckle cracking and something slammed into the side of my head. I looked down and thought I was falling, but it was only oblivion reaching up for me.

A lucky kick, sneaky. I wasn't out for long and when I saw my attacker's bloody fingerprints on the roof I felt almost better. I was in better shape than him. Better dressed too; his torn jacket lay on the roof beside me. I laughed and sat up and then I didn't feel good at all. I grabbed the jacket and lay down again.

A little later I looked down into the lane which was empty. I congratulated myself on protecting Swan from the garbage. That was why I was up on the roof wasn't it? *Good job, Cliff,* I thought. *Let's have a drink*. Then I looked at the jacket clutched in my hand and remembered that there was a little more to it than that.

It was a cheap jacket, and it had nearly caused its shoplifting, garbage-throwing owner to fall six storeys. Worse, it had a piece of paper in a pocket with his name and address on it. George Pagemill of 537 22nd Street had had the brakes checked and the tyres rotated on his 1969 Plymouth at a local service station.

I went by my hotel, picked up my .38 and took a taxi to 22nd Street east of the railway. A rusty blue Plymouth was in the street outside 537, which was an old house divided into apartments and rooms. George was in room eight at the top of a dark set of stairs and opposite a gurgling toilet. The toilet was empty and the doorlock was the same as George's, a cheap job that wouldn't have deterred a determined Girl Guide. I listened and heard muttering inside. I held the gun in my left hand, crouched a bit and drove my right shoulder up and into the door opposite the lock. The lock broke, the door flew open and I spun into the room, changing hands on the gun as I came.

George was sitting on the bed with a beer can held gingerly in his taped-up hands. It seemed to be taking all his strength to lift it. I pushed the door shut with my foot. The heavy stuff so soon after the fun and games on the roof had made my head throb. I felt mean.

'Hi, George.'

He gaped at the gun. 'Hey,' he said weakly.

'Aren't you going to talk to Jesus?'

I chopped the can out of his hands with the muzzle of the gun; beer sprayed over his pants and the bed. I put the gun away and swept a quick look around the room—walnut veneer furniture, a stained hand basin under a dusty window, linoleum on the floor. George was no Mr Big. He was as seedy as the room, with a thin, defeated face that was just waiting to get old.

'Get outta here.' His voice was flat and dull; his heart wasn't in it.

'Whose idea was it to throw the garbage?'

He shook his head and put his bandaged fingers together. He rubbed them tenderly like a man who doesn't expect to be hurt.

'I could put you in for assault,' I said.

'Bullshit.'

'I've got an armload of books with your prints all over them. Shoplifting.'

'Crap. Anyone can look at books, open them and everything.'

I stepped close enough to smell him, reached across and opened and closed a drawer on the chest experimentally. A smell of dirty shirt came up.

'I could break your fingers.'

'Why?'

'Why what?'

'Why would you break my fingers?'

'Because you're being strong and silent about who got you to throw the garbage. You've got a choice, George; are you more afraid of him or me?'

He glanced up and I gave him my hard look.

'You,' he said.

'All right.'

'Bookstore guy. I met him in a bar. He offered me a hundred bucks to do it for a month.'

'Shoplift and throw garbage?'

'Yeah. He didn't say why.'

'Why'd you dump the books?'

He looked at me as if I'd asked him to state the theory of relativity as an equation. 'What else would I do with them?'

I took the gun out and looked at it. 'Your contract is cancelled as of now, got it?'

He nodded.

'I suggest you stay here for awhile. An hour say. I might be on the street I might not. You better play it safe.'

He nodded again and I opened the door.

'Hey,' he whined, 'where's my jacket?'

'On the roof with the other garbage.'

The first thing I did was call Swan.

'Where's Milt?' I said.

'Here.'

'If he gets a phone call, stall him, I'm on my way.'

I called a cab, telling the operator it was urgent. The taxi came quickly and moved fast through the thin mid-afternoon traffic. I sprinted down the alley to Swan's door. He opened it and put a finger to his lips.

'He says he's sick. He got a call. Wants to go home.'

'Let him. Has he got a car here?'

'I suppose. Why?'

'Have you got one?'

'I can borrow something.'

'Something?'

'A motor cycle.'

'Shit.'

'With a sidecar.'

'Oh, Jesus. All right. Can you leave now?'

'Sure, Maggie's here.' He ducked back through the door, shouted 'Okay, Milt!' down the steps and came back.

'Out here.' He led me down towards a dumpster in the alley. Beside it was his motor cycle, an old Harley Davidson. The sidecar was a World War Two relic with patches on the fabric and dents like bullet holes in the body.

'Has Milton-Smith ever seen you on this?'

He pulled out heavy goggles and a helmet like Lindbergh's. 'No. Friend in the next building lets me use it, but I don't need it much.'

I levered myself into the sidecar which was as comfortable as a coffin. The motor caught at Swan's first kick and we puttered down the alley. Up the street Milton-Smith was trotting along on his short legs towards a garage. We stopped with a clear view of the exit and waited. After ten minutes, a green Dodge Dart rolled out.

'That's him,' Swan said.

'Follow that car.'

The Dart crossed Market Street and began the manoeuvres designed to put it on a high road leading north-east. The wind was roaring and cold, and I only had a T-shirt and a light velour sweater between me and it.

'Where's he going?' I shouted.

'Oakland, Berkeley ...' The wind whipped the words away.

I was disappointed, not the Golden Gate. The traffic moved fast but Swan was a good rider and he kept the bike steady and my sidecar out of harm's way. I was starting to enjoy the ride when he waved and shouted at me.

'What?'

'Toll.'

I fished out coins and scattered them into the machine like birdseed. The Dart had got a smoother passage through and Swan had to change lanes and pick up speed to stay in touch. The sidecar swayed and I felt like a flightless fledgling teetering on a branch.

Milt took a north-going turn off the bridge and Swan mouthed Berkeley at me. I thought about communes, marches, protests, but the streets were quiet and there wasn't an untrimmed beard in sight. The Dart made a few turns and slid into a parking lot attached to a building with tinted glass, white pebbles and potted palms. Swan slammed on the brakes and the edge of the sidecar took me hard and low on the rib cage. I climbed out swearing, said 'Wait' ill-naturedly and hobbled off to where the sliding doors were closing behind Milton-Smith's narrow shoulders and sticking-out bum.

Inside it was dark enough to screen *Casablanca* When my eyes got used to the gloom I saw Milt waiting by the elevators with a flock of secretaries carrying files and folders. He was impatient, shifting from foot to foot, and nervous, scratching at his thinly covered skull. We all piled into the elevator and I lined up behind Milt as he touched button six.

At six he got out, turned left and walked down a short corridor. I hung back and watched him go into an office marked Palmer F. Wong—Realty & Investments. I hung around for fifteen minutes and no one went in or out of the office. Milt was in conference.

Back on the street, I filled Swan in.

'What does it mean?' he said.

'Don't know. He loses money to Chinese gambling, and here he is ensconced with a Chinese money man after getting a phone call from a guy he hired to harass you. It has to hang together somehow.'

'We could shake it out of him,' Swan said.

Just then Milton-Smith came out of the building. Swan ducked his head and fiddled with his goggles but I took a good long look. The man with Milt was about six foot four and couldn't have weighed less than two hundred pounds. He had a shaven skull and only one ear; the other side of his head was just smooth, waxed, yellow skin. He took long bouncy strides as if he liked to feel the sidewalk under his feet. I wondered what else he could do with his feet.

Swan had shot them a quick look. 'Guess not,' he said.

'No.'

'Well, the answer's there, in that building.'

I sighed. 'Yeah, I know. You better go home. I'll call you in the morning.'

I was cold and tired by the time I had a fix on the security arrangements for what I was privately calling the Wong building. The place basically emptied at 5 o'clock with a few over-achievers hanging around till six or a little past. A security patrol van came by at seven; an armed man looked for lights, used a telephone in the lobby and then locked up. The van came back at nine; a guard checked the front door, a side service door and the small underground parking lot.

I walked a couple of blocks to get warm, called a cab and went back to the city. I had a late dinner near the hotel and crawled into bed not looking forward to the next day, and wondering why I didn't just chuck it and fly back to Sydney. I knew why—I liked Swan, I'd taken his money and I wanted to know what was going on.

'I thought you were going to do it last night,' Swan said when I called him.

'That shows how much you know about the detective business. It's tonight. Milt in today?'

'Yeah.'

'How's he looking?'

'Nervous.'

'You see that big Chinese with the one ear?'

'No.'

'That's right, you wouldn't. I'll call you again tonight.'

I spent the early afternoon buying a few things. At 4 o'clock I was back at the Wong building in Berkeley. By 4.40 I was lying across the beams inside the acoustic tiles, maybe two metres above the toilets, in the men's room on the sixth floor. I'd used the toilet before I'd climbed up into the space which was about half the size of a telephone booth. Among my effects I had a flask of whisky and a strong flashlight. I'd wound my watch.

The time passed slowly and it was hard not to sneeze. I climbed down at 6.45 and snuck a look down the corridors. There was a light near the elevator, otherwise the whole floor was dark. At 7 o'clock, phones started ringing; one rang on every floor and then there was silence. Working by the flashlight, it took me ten minutes to get in Mr Wong's secretary's room and another five to get into the inner sanctum. In the strong beam I picked out individual objects—a big, tidy desk, a wet bar, chairs, two filing cabinets.

Filing cabinets are a pushover and some systematiser had made it easy for me. The first cabinet contained a folder labelled SWAN. I took it over to the desk, sat down and went through it. The song it sang was clear if not sweet. Daniel Swan had filed a number of preservation requests on San Francisco buildings with the Heritage Committee and the City Hall when he began working as a tour guide. From his hastily written letter to the City, with the building designations filled in by hand, it seemed that this was a routine procedure. The applications had been put on open review by the

City, which effectively blocked applications to demolish or substantially alter the said buildings. A proposal by Fenner A. Wong for a re-development of the Baltimore Building site had been refused, with Swan's preservation request cited as the grounds.

I looked in vain for Milt under 'M' but I found him under 'S'. He owed Kwong-Ping Wong of Washington Street slightly more than fifteen thousand dollars, and had taken out an unsecured loan with Palmer F. Wong for just that amount.

I used the Nashua copier in the outer office to make several copies of all documents, put the files back and locked up after me. At the bottom of the fire stairs was a door with a padlock on it which led out to the car park. I was ready for padlocks and this one didn't give me any trouble.

A light showed into O'Farrell Street from the shop. I rattled the door and Swan opened it with the hand that wasn't holding money.

'How's the take?'

'Lousy.'

We went back to the register, stepping over the boxes and weaving between the untidy tables.

'Your troubles are over,' I said. 'Or maybe they're just starting.' I laid out the documents on the counter. Swan got two beers from his loft and took a long swig before reading. I remembered my flask and had a shot and a chaser. He started to smile on the third page and it had spread, broad and winning across his narrow, dark features by the time he'd finished.

'Shit,' he said and drained his can, 'I'd forgotten those preservation requests.'

'Very enlightening. Why the grin?'

He picked up one of the photocopy sheets and rustled it. 'It's the wrong building.'

'What is?'

'This one, the Baltimore. A magazine writer nominated it as the Fat Man's hotel and I went along with him when I was just starting out. I put in a request on it, but I know better now. It doesn't fit. I haven't taken the tour past there in a year. Didn't you notice, Hardy? Couldn't have been paying attention. I can lift that request tomorrow.'

'What about the building?'

'An eyesore. Wong can call Milt off. Say, he must be the one stole my bird. Hardy . . . can you . . . ?'

I had another shot and put the whisky away. 'Sure,' I said, 'might as well. Where's the phone book? Here's what we do.'

Milt lived in South San Francisco and my third cab of the day made a sizable hole in Swan's tour money. If everything worked out, I planned to hit him for the expenses. I could give him the burglar's tools for a keepsake. It was a bland, anonymous street and a bland anonymous apartment block, the kind of place you go to once and forget forever. I unshipped the .38 and stuck it up the Chinese's wide, flaring nose when he opened the door.

'Back up,' I said. 'Let's go to where the phone is. It's going to ring soon.'

He looked at me carefully and seemed to decide it would be worthwhile letting me live a few minutes longer. I followed him down a hallway to a small living room where Milt was sitting at a table with a pack of tarot cards laid out in front of him. He looked up at me with his struggling thought processes showing on his gnomish face.

'In the shop,' I said. '*Canticle for Liebowitz*, and in Kwong-Ping's on Washington, and in the elevator to Mr Wong's office.'

Bewilderment followed puzzlement and I felt sorry for him. The Chinese loomed against a bookshelf filled with Sci-Fi paperbacks and if I hadn't known he was inscrutable I'd have thought he was impatient. The phone rang.

'Answer it,' I said to the Chinese. 'It's for you.'

He picked up the receiver and listened to the fast, sing-song words. He spoke once, put the phone down, picked up a coat and hat from a chair and walked out.

Milton-Smith looked down at the tarot cards, then turned his watery pale-blue eyes on me.

'I don't understand,' he said.

I put the gun away and turned over one of the cards. 'It's pretty simple, Milt. Dan Swan talked to Mr Wong tonight and they've settled their differences. That means I'm not interested in George Pagemill anymore, or in you. That means Mr Wong calls off Odd Job there. You've still got your gambling debts and your loan and I'd think you were out a job. But that's your problem.'

He sighed and moved a card with a bitten-to-the-quick fingernail.

'Where's the bird?' I said.

He pointed down to a cupboard under a bookcase. I reached down and opened it. The figure was wrapped in a grey rag that had once been an undervest. It was about a foot high, shiny black, and weighed about the same as a full bottle of beer.

'Why'd you keep it?'

He shrugged, then something like hope flickered across his face. 'Dan'll be glad to get it back, won't he? You think he might let me keep my job?'

'He just might,' I said. 'He seems like a pretty nice guy.'

'The Big Drop' (as 'Blue Money'), 'P.I. Blues' (as 'Angel of Death'), 'What Would You Do?' (as 'The Big Knot'), 'The Big Pinch' and 'Maltese Falcon' have previously appeared in *Penthouse*; 'The Arms of the Law' was originally published in *People*; 'The Mongol Scroll' was originally published in *Playboy*; and 'The Mae West Scam' was originally published in *Follow Me*.